By Phil Bildner

The Rip and Red Series

A Whole New Ballgame
Rookie of the Year
Tournament of Champions
Most Valuable Players

The Sluggers Series
with Loren Long

Magic in the Outfield
Horsin' Around
Great Balls of Fire
Water, Water Everywhere
Blastin' the Blues
Home of the Brave

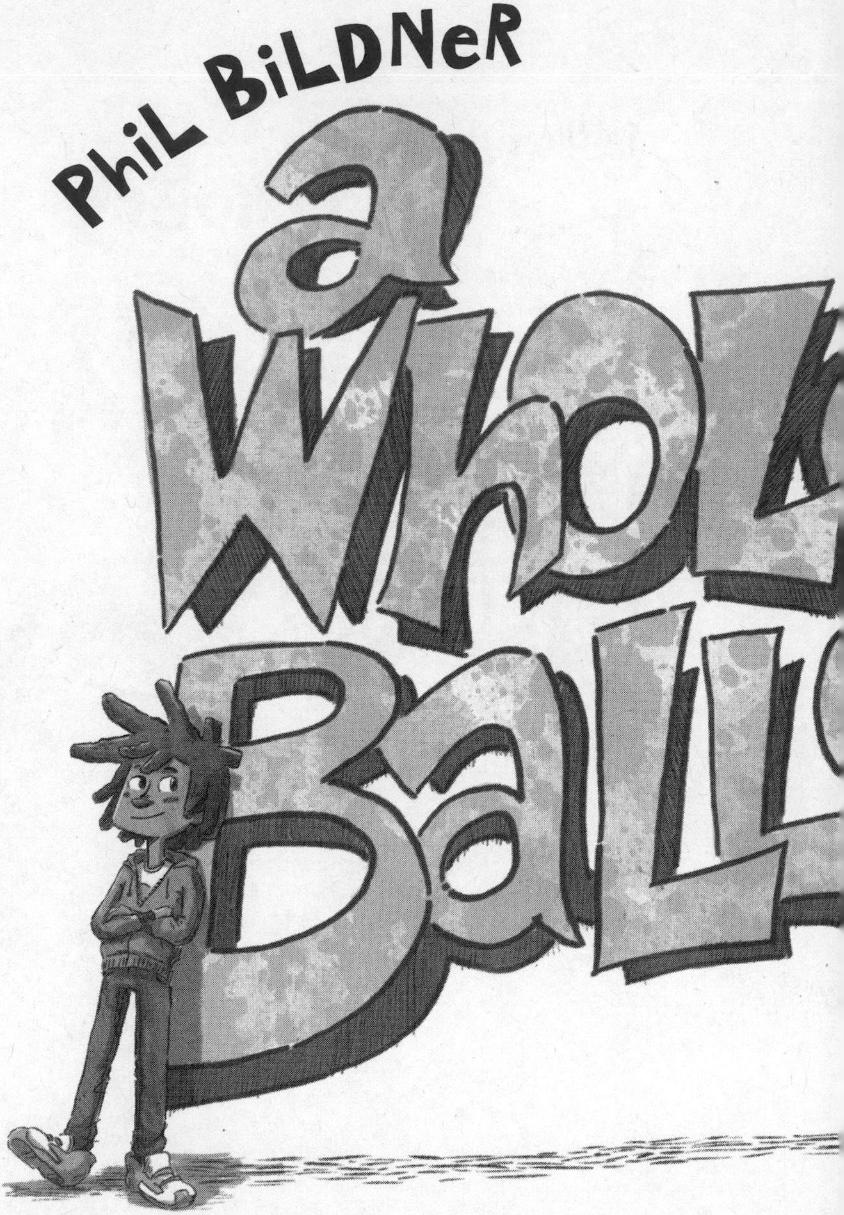
PHIL BILDNER

pictures by TiM PROBeRt

New
game

SQUARE
FISH

Farrar Straus Giroux
New York

SQUARE
FISH

An imprint of Macmillan Publishing Group, LLC
175 Fifth Avenue
New York, NY 10010
mackids.com

Our books may be purchased in bulk for promotional, educational, or business
use. Please contact your local bookseller or the Macmillan Corporate and
Premium Sales Department at (800) 221-7945 ext. 5442 or by
e-mail at MacmillanSpecialMarkets@macmillan.com.

Library of Congress Cataloging-in-Publication Data
Bildner, Phil.
    A whole new ballgame : a Rip and Red story / Phil Bildner ; pictures
by Tim Probert.
        pages cm
    Summary: "From the first morning with their odd new teacher fifth
grade is full of shocking surprises for best friends Rip and Red"—Provided
by publisher.
    ISBN 978-1-250-07976-3 (paperback)   ISBN 978-0-374-30133-0 (ebook)
    [1. Teachers—Fiction. 2. Schools—Fiction. 3. Best friends—Fiction.
4. Friendship—Fiction.] I. Probert, Tim, illustrator. II. Title.

PZ7.B4923Who 2015
[Fic]—dc23
                                                                2014040150

Originally published in the United States by Farrar Straus Giroux
First Square Fish Edition: 2016
Book designed by Andrew Arnold
Square Fish logo designed by Filomena Tuosto

13   15   17   19   20   18   16   14

AR: 5.0 / LEXILE: 540L

For Erin

Fifth Grade!

I **bolted toward** the chain-link fence. Red shot for the gate. In full stride, I slipped my backpack down my shoulders, and as soon as Red grabbed the metal post and spun into the schoolyard, I flung the bag over the fence.

Red caught it by the straps just before it touched the grass.

"Boo-yah!" I hammer-fisted the air.

"Bam!" He held it up. "Every time, Mason Irving!"

Mason Irving. That's what Red calls me. Everyone else calls me by my nickname, Rip.

I held out my fist. Red gave me a pound.

At 7:25 every morning, I meet Red at the end of his driveway, and we walk to Reese Jones Elementary. Orleans Lane to Key Place to Niagara Drive. Then when we get to RJE, I toss my bag, Red catches it, and we zigzag through the portables—the second- and third-grade classrooms—and head for the new playground.

It's our walk-to-school routine. Red likes routines.

But this morning wasn't like other mornings. Because today was the first day of fifth grade.

Fifth grade!

At RJE, all the fifth graders have Ms. Hamburger, and yes, that's her real name, and no, I'm not going to make any jokes, because if you go to RJE, you've heard them all. Ms. Hamburger's been teaching fifth grade ever since RJE opened twenty-five years ago.

"I hope Ms. Hamburger lets us sit at the same table," Red said.

"Me, too."

"I heard she assigns seats at the beginning of the year."

I grabbed the granola bar from my jeans pocket, snapped off a piece, and flipped it to Red.

"I hope Ms. Hamburger lets us bring snacks to class," he said. "I hope she lets us keep water bottles at our table."

We reached the walkway to the playground.

"You ready?" I said.

"Ready as I'll ever be, Mason Irving."

I shook out my hair and brushed back the locks above my ears. "On your mark, get set . . ."

"Go!"

We whipped our bags onto the benches and tore across the sand toward the jungle gym. We speed-walked the balance beam and then split up—Red darted for the climbing wall; I went for the monkey bars. I swung across the rungs, two-at-a-timed the steps to the upper deck, and

waited for Red. Then we dove for the spiral slide. I went down first.

"Boo-yah!" I shouted.

"Bam!" Red followed.

Obstacle-coursing the jungle gym is another part of our walk-to-school routine, our favorite part.

We scooped up our bags, and as we left the playground, we tapped the wooden posts with the solar lights. Two summers ago, when the community built the playground, Red and I helped put in those posts.

I pulled the granola bar wrapper from my pocket and crumpled it tight.

"Irving with the crossover dribble," I said, pretending to announce the play-by-play. I made a move for the garbage. "He stutter-steps toward the key . . . breaks right . . . shoots . . . nothing but the bottom of the can! Oh, what a move by Rip!"

"We're playing basketball," Red sang—the intro song from Xbox. "We love that basketball."

Basketball.

Not only was today the first day of fifth grade, but it was also the first day of the fifth-grade basketball program. Red and I were playing hoops together for the first time.

Until now, Red hadn't been allowed to play hoops at school.

We turned onto the sidewalk in front of the school and headed up the circular drive. Like always, we timed our arrival perfectly, reaching the doors just as the first buses pulled up and the first bikers and scooter riders pulled into the racks.

Red likes being on time. He does better when he's on time.

"Where's Ms. Darling?" he asked, tightening his fists into knots. He shook them next to his eyes. "Where's . . . where's Ms. Waldon?"

I looked around. "I don't know."

The principal, Ms. Darling—yes, that's her real name, too—always stood between the double doors, saying good morning and telling kids, "Take off your hats when you enter the building." Ms. Waldon, the parent coordinator, always sat at the desk under the announcement monitor in the main hall.

But not today.

We strutted down the K-1 hallway—fifth graders strut, especially down the K-1 hallway—and then headed up the stairs by the bathrooms.

The K-1 hallway staircase is the only staircase Red uses.

On the second floor, we passed the library and sped up as we got closer to Room 208, Ms. Hamburger's room.

"You ready?" I asked.

"Ready as I'll ever be, Mason Irving."

When I reached the doorway, I stopped dead in my tracks.

The person standing in front of the classroom was *not* Ms. Hamburger.

Mr. Acevedo

A man stood at the front of Room 208.

He looked like a cross between the barista at Perky's, the coffee shop my mom always complains about because it's so expensive (even though she stops there every morning), and the bassist from Elephant Sponges, this band I saw on You-Tube. The man had long, dark hair, piercings up and down both ears, and braided leather bracelets.

I checked Red. His shoulder brushed against mine, and he'd turtled his neck like he was hiding. He tapped his thigh—pinky-thumb-pinky-thumb-pinky-thumb-pinky-thumb—real fast.

When Red's nervous, he pinky-thumbs his leg.

"You okay?" I said softly.

"Where's Ms. Hamburger?"

"I don't know."

"Is Ms. Hamburger still our teacher? Where's Ms. Hamburger?"

"We'll find out."

The man motioned for us to come in.

The desks were arranged in tables, four seats at each, and since Red and I were first to arrive, we had dibs. I tapped him on the arm and led us to the front table on the far side. We sat down with our backs to the window.

Red likes to face the door.

"Who is that?" He hunched forward.

"Not sure."

"Where's Ms. Hamburger?" His knees bounced against the underside of his desk.

I placed my hand on his leg.

I can touch Red. So can a few grown-ups. But Red doesn't really like it when people touch him.

The other kids began to arrive:

Melissa dropped her volleyball and checked the number on the door three times before walking in. Bryan back-pedaled to the table in front of the cubbies. Diego swung the tie strings on his knit hat, raised his grab-and-go breakfast bag, and then headed for a seat in the middle of the room.

Melissa, Bryan, Diego—I know all the kids. All the fifth graders know one another. How could we not? We've been together our entire time at RJE.

But we're the last one-class grade. All the lower grades have three or four classes, which is why the portables now take up half of the schoolyard.

The man at the front of the room didn't say a word until Avery rolled in.

"Do you have enough room?" he said. He took a step toward her wheelchair and then backed away.

She curled her lip. "Who are you?"

"Where do you prefer to sit?"

"Prefer? Are you the teacher or something?"

"I'll explain once everyone's here."

"Whatever, dude." She wheeled next to Melissa, pulled out the chair, and parked.

"I think that's about everyone," the man said. He glanced at the clock by the door and then reached for the iPad in the pen tray of the board. "Day one and all twenty-six of you are ready to go before the bell. Outstanding."

He tucked his hair behind his ears and looked at each table.

"I'm Mr. Acevedo," he said, tapping his chest. "I'm going to be your homeroom and Language Arts—ELA—teacher this year. Starting today, we'll be spending the first one hundred twenty minutes of every school day together. Well, except for today. We have early dismissal today. So we only get sixty minutes today."

Suddenly, Mr. Acevedo leaped into the air and kicked together the heels of his high-tops. But on the way down, his toe caught the back of Olivia's chair, and he stumbled into the shelf of red binders next to the board.

"OMG!" Olivia shouted.

"Sick!" Danny said.

Red grabbed my shoulder and ducked behind me.

Some kids laughed.

Mr. Acevedo steadied the shelf and then rushed over to Olivia. "Are you okay? Did I kick you?"

She shook her head.

"Phew." Mr. Acevedo cringed. "Awkward."

"I'll say," Trinity said.

More kids laughed.

Slowly, Red sat back up, but his knees still knocked against his desk.

"Thank you." Mr. Acevedo waved his iPad like a performer waving to the audience. "Thank you very much." With his other hand, he brushed some hair off his face. "This is my very first day as a teacher, so I wanted to do something memorable. But now I'm thinking I probably should've practiced that jump once or twice before giving it a whirl in front of everyone."

"I'll say," Trinity said again.

More kids laughed.

"Well, look at it this way." Mr. Acevedo shrugged. "I guarantee you'll never forget your first moments of fifth grade—when your new teacher nearly face-planted in front of the class."

He swiped his screen, took a moment to read, and then placed the iPad back in the tray.

"Before we get started here," he said, "let's get some of the basics out of the way. First, I'm not a big fan of homework. You won't be getting much from me."

"That's what I'm talking about!" Jordan said, shaking his thumb and index finger at Bryan across his table. "I like this guy already."

A few kids clapped.

"Second," Mr. Acevedo said, holding up two fingers, "I'm not a big fan of worksheets. In fact, I *hate* worksheets. Now I know we're not supposed to use the H-word here at RJE, but when it comes to worksheets, I make an exception. There will be no worksheets in this classroom."

He picked up a poster tube from the floor by the board, slide-stepped to the door, and peeked into the hall. Then he charged across the room and leaped onto his desk, which was next to our table.

"I hereby declare our classroom an NWZ!" He raised the tube and posed like Thor. "This room is a No Worksheet Zone." He pried off the end, shook out the bright orange poster, and unrolled it.

"I'll hang this later," he said. He hopped down. "What else?" He placed the poster and tube on his desk and headed back to the front of the room. "Oh, you see these jeans?" He brushed his legs. "I'll be wearing them pretty much every day. So if you want to make fun of that, go right ahead. But rest assured, I do change my shirt, socks, and underwear daily. I also shower and brush my teeth regularly. I expect that you will do the same. Our classroom will not be pungent, and if you don't know what *pungent* means, look it up."

I'm pretty sure I knew what *pungent* meant. Mom calls my sneakers pungent when I wear them without socks over the summer and they stink up my whole room.

I checked Red. His feet were flat on the floor, his eyes fixed on Mr. Acevedo.

"Phew, I'm gassed." Mr. Acevedo headed for his desk again. "I say we take a break. I'm a big fan of breaks. We learn more effectively when we take breaks. So for the next fifteen minutes, feel free to do what you like—read, write, draw, talk to your classmates, find your cubbies, put your belongings away. Just remember, you're in fifth grade now. You know how to behave in a classroom. I don't have to go over that."

I was glad he wasn't going to lecture us. I got enough of that at home.

Mr. Acevedo opened his top desk drawer and pulled out a book. "For the next fifteen minutes, I'm reading." He reached back into the drawer and pulled out another sign. This one he hung around his neck:

Rip and Red

Fifteen minutes later...

Mr. Acevedo closed his book and took off the sign.

"Let's do a little housekeeping," he said, heading back to the front of the class. "There are twenty-six of you in here, and right now I don't know any of your names. That needs to change quickly." He swiped the screen. "Let's do the attendance thing. Who's my first victim?"

"I am," Jordan called out.

"Are you Jordan Adams?"

"Uh-huh."

"You thought you were my first victim because your last name starts with *A*?"

"Uh-huh."

"Well, Jordan Adams, you're not my first victim. I'm not an alphabetical teacher. My last name's Acevedo. When I was in school, I had to go first way too many times. Alphabetical is boring and predictable. I don't like boring and predictable. I like exciting and unpredictable." He tightened an earring. "Anyway, when I asked who wanted to be my first victim, I meant it more as a rhetorical question, and if you don't know what *rhetorical question* means, look it up."

I'm pretty sure I knew what *rhetorical question* meant. It's one of those fake questions you're not really supposed to answer.

"When I call your name," Mr. Acevedo said, "please raise your hand, and let me know what you want to be called. What name do you prefer? Then tell me something about yourself. Something serious, something funny, something kooky, whatever you want. One thing." He peeked at his screen. "Where's Sebastian King?"

Sebastian raised his hand. "Call me Sebi."

"Sebi it is. Tell me one thing about yourself, Sebi."

"I like to doodle and draw."

"I'm a doodler, too." Mr. Acevedo patted his chest. "Feel free to doodle away in here. Xander McDonald?"

Xander sat next to Sebi. He raised his hand. "Call me X."

"Is anyone in your family going to beat me up if I do?"

"I hope not."

"I hope not, too. X it is. What's your one thing, X?"

"I love the Beatles." He lifted up his sweatshirt and pulled down his Beatles tee.

Mr. Acevedo swiped the screen. "Blake Daniels?"

"I'm Blake Daniels." Red's hand shot up. "Everyone calls me Red. So you should call me Blake Daniels. I mean . . ." He covered his face with his hands. "You should call . . . you should call me Red. Call me Red."

"Red it is. I take it people call you Red because of your hair?"

Red nodded. His knees bounced against his desk.

Red has thick blondish-red hair. It covers his ears and neck. Red doesn't comb his hair very often.

"So what's your one thing, Red?"

Red moved his hands from his face. "I don't like it when people touch my hair."

"I don't like when people touch my hair either," Mr. Acevedo said. "Give me another one, Red."

Red's fingers snapped back to his cheeks. "Another what?" He swayed his shoulders from side to side.

"Another one thing," Mr. Acevedo said. "Tell me something else. What's another one thing?"

Red clasped his hands behind his neck, hunched his shoulders, and squeezed his head with his arms. That's what Red does when he's nervous and confused. Sometimes he squinches his face real tight, wrinkling his eyes, nose, and forehead. I call that Red's old-man face.

I don't like Red's old-man face.

"Say something basketball," I whispered.

"What?" Red glanced at me, looked back to Mr. Acevedo, and then faced me again.

"Say something about the Warriors."

Red moved his elbows from his head and turned back to Mr. Acevedo. "The Golden State Warriors are my favorite basketball team," he said.

Mr. Acevedo pumped his fist. I held out mine to Red.

Slowly, Red lowered his hands and touched my knuckles.

Half a pound was better than no pound.

"I hope I get this one right," Mr. Acevedo said. "Mariam . . . Tehrani?"

"That's right," Mariam said. She pointed to Olivia and Grace across her table. "You can call us OMG."

"Why's that?" Mr. Acevedo asked.

"Because of our names," Mariam said. "Olivia's starts with *O*, mine starts with *M*, and Grace's starts with *G*. OMG."

"BFFs," Mr. Acevedo said. "And what's your one thing, Mariam?"

"I love scary movies and ghost stories. Wait. Is that one thing or two?"

"We'll count it as one. Mason Irving?"

I raised my hand. "Call me Rip."

"Why Rip?"

"It's a basketball nickname."

"Rip it is. Rip and Red, sitting next to each other. I like that. Easy for me to remember. What's your one thing, Rip?"

I smiled. "I don't like when people touch my hair."

"You don't, Mason Irving?" Red said, puzzled.

"Just playin'."

"Well, I would understand if you didn't," Mr. Acevedo said. "A buddy of mine has dreadlocks like yours. No one's allowed to go near them."

Up until last year, I always buzzed my head, or should I say, my mom always buzzed my head. I only started growing my hair in fourth grade.

"So what's your one thing, Rip?" Mr. Acevedo asked.

"I do basketball play-by-play."

"Fascinating. I hope I get to hear you."

* * *

"Now that we've gotten that out of the way," Mr. Acevedo said after he finished taking attendance, "let's . . ."

Xander's hand shot up.

"Yes, X?" Mr. Acevedo pointed.

"Where's Ms. Hamburger?"

Other kids raised their hands.

Mr. Acevedo motioned to Gavin.

"Where was Ms. Darling this morning?" he asked. "Is she still the principal?"

"Is Ms. Waldon still the parent coordinator?" Attie called out.

Mr. Acevedo pointed with his chin to Trinity.

"If you're only our ELA teacher," she said, "who are our other teachers?"

"Are we switching classes?" Attie called out again.

"Wow. Questions, questions, questions," Mr. Acevedo said. "I'll answer all of them. I promise. But not until tomorrow. We only have about ten minutes left today, and I really want to finish this chapter." He held up the book he was reading during the break. "But I will answer Attie's last question. Yes, you are switching classes."

"Where do we go?" she asked.

"I'll let you know on your way out. But right now, these pages are calling to me." He knocked the cover. "Please make sure you have something to read in here at all times. I don't care what you're reading, so long as you're reading something. In Room 208, we're committed to reading. We're committed to reading every day." He picked up his do-not-disturb sign, slipped it around his neck, and sat cross-legged on his desk. "Tune in tomorrow for another exciting episode of *Room 208, Unexpected*."

Slammed!

"I feel like I got hit by a bus," I said, twisting a lock near my forehead at its root.

"How do you know what it feels like to get hit by a bus?" Red asked.

We were in the cafeteria, sitting in a fifth-graders-only booth along the sidewall.

"I mean by Mr. Acevedo," I said.

"Mr. Acevedo drives a bus?"

I let out a puff. "It's an expression, Red. It means getting hit hard or slammed."

"Got it. Hit by a bus."

I stared at my tray. Most days, I wolfed down my lunch. But today, I didn't touch it. I was still trying to digest the morning. "Where'd you go after ELA?" I twisted another lock.

"I was with Ms. Yvonne," Red said, spinning his empty tray. "Ms. Yvonne says things are going to be very different this year. Ms. Yvonne doesn't have her schedule yet. She's going to let me know her schedule as soon as she gets it."

Ms. Yvonne is a special ed teacher. She's worked with Red ever since pre-K. All the fifth graders know Ms. Yvonne. Whenever she's in the classroom, she tries to help everyone, not just the kids who get services.

"Are you going to eat your Super Salad featuring chilled chicken tender strips, crispy green lettuce, and freshly diced tomatoes?" Red asked.

Red always describes the school lunch word-for-word from the announcement monitor.

I slid him the tray. He scarfed down my lunch.

Ready to Ball

"You almost done in there?" I asked.

"One minute," Red said.

We were in the boys' bathroom on the K-1 hallway. Red was in the middle stall, the only one he'll use at RJE. I was sitting on the sink, checking my scalp in the mirror.

"When Coach Lebo and those varsity kids see you shoot free throws," I said, "you're going to blow their minds."

Red is the best foul shooter I've ever seen. One time, in the schoolyard, he sank forty-four in a row. Yeah, forty-four in a row.

Coach Lebo coaches the Clifton High School varsity basketball team. Twice a week during the fall and spring, he brings the varsity and junior varsity players down to RJE for the fifth-grade basketball program.

"I'm done, Mason Irving," Red said, opening the door.

"You're wearing the exact same thing."

"No, I'm not." He showed me the clothes in his bag. "This is a different shirt. These are different shorts."

Red only wears shorts. Never jeans, never long pants, no matter the weather. He never wears anything clingy or itchy either. Definitely never anything itchy.

I slid off the sink and ripped a paper towel from the dispenser.

"Irving holds for one," I play-by-played. I crumpled the towel and sized up the garbage by the door. "Six seconds on the clock . . . Irving eyes his defender. Fakes left . . . jukes right . . . driving down the lane . . ." I flicked the towel toward the can. "Finger roll!"

But the towel didn't make it over the lip. It fell to the floor.

Red pounced.

"Bam!" he shouted as he overhead-slammed it into the trash. He pinched out the Warriors logo on his shirt.

"Let's go play some real ball," I said.

We headed out past the kindergarten classrooms and turned down the main hall. Even before we got to the cafeteria, we could hear the squeaking sneakers and bouncing balls.

"It sounds like everyone's here," Red said.

"Do you have your earplugs?" I asked.

He patted his pocket.

Red doesn't like loud noises. Sometimes he wears noise-canceling headphones or earplugs.

We speed-walked through the cafeteria toward the gym door. When I pulled it open, I stopped dead in my tracks.

Mr. Acevedo stood in the middle of the gym.

Huh?

Mr. Acevedo stood in the middle of the gym twirling his whistle like a lifeguard.

"What's going on?" Red slid behind me. "Where's Coach Lebo?"

"Where are all the high school kids?" I asked.

The gym was packed, but not with the varsity and junior varsity players. The gym was packed with fifth graders— boys *and* girls—from all the Clifton elementary schools. I recognized most of them from spring soccer. From RJE, Jordan and Noah were shooting at the hoop near the locker rooms. Christine and Isa were at the basket by the stage.

"Why are all these kids here?" Red turtled his neck. "Where's Coach Lebo?"

"I don't know."

"Rip and Red," Mr. Acevedo called. He snatched his whistle and started toward us.

"Look at all his tattoos," Red said.

I already was.

Mr. Acevedo's arms and legs were covered in ink. On his right arm, there were musical symbols and notes. On his left, there was something written in cursive. His leg tats were all different colors. On his right leg, there was a flag. On his left, butterflies.

"More familiar faces," Mr. Acevedo said, walking up. "Excellent."

"Where's Coach Lebo?" I asked.

"What are you doing here, Mr. Acevedo?" Red pinky-thumbed his leg. "Where are the high school kids?"

"Questions, questions, questions." Mr. Acevedo twirled his whistle again. "I'll answer them in a few minutes. Glad you two made it." He headed off.

I turned to Red.

He was gone.

Handshake

I tore out of the gym and into the cafeteria. I spotted Red right away, sitting at the same booth from lunch.

"What happened?" I said, hurrying over.

He was hunched forward with his hands clasped behind his neck and his elbows vise-gripping his head. His knees knocked against the underside of the table.

"Red, what happened?" I sat down across from him.

He didn't answer. He just shook his head and stared off.

I checked the gym door. Mr. Acevedo hadn't seen Red run out, and I was pretty sure he hadn't seen me leave either. But he would definitely notice if we weren't there for the start.

"What happened?" I asked again.

"I don't know," Red said softly, still shaking his head. "I don't know, I don't know."

"Let's go back in and play ball."

"I don't know, I don't know."

"Come on, Red."

"I don't know, Mason Irving. Where's Coach Lebo? Why are all those kids in there?"

"Let's go back in and find out."

"Where's Coach Lebo?"

I checked the gym door again and then tapped the table. "We need a handshake," I said, standing up.

"A handshake?"

"Yeah, a handshake. We're finally playing ball together, Red. We need our own handshake. Stand up."

He slid out of the booth.

Together, we came up with a handshake:

> Right-handed high-five.
> Left-handed high-five.
> Right elbow-bash, left elbow-bash.
> Right-hand slap, front and back.
> Left-hand slap, front and back.
> Top fist, top fist, knock fists, blow it up.
> Three-sixty turn, jumping hip bump. Then
>   on the landing . . .
> "Boo-yah!"

We nailed it the first time.

"Put in your earplugs," I said.

Red pulled them from his pocket and put them in.

"You ready?" I said.

"Ready as I'll ever be, Mason Irving."

Coach Acevedo

Tweet! Tweet!

"Let's huddle up!" Mr. Acevedo called from center court. He waited for everyone to get close. "Let's hold the balls, please." He pointed to the kids still dribbling. "Not while I'm talking."

Tweet! Tweet!

"I get a little whistle happy," he said, smiling. "Get used to it."

Tweet! Tweet!

"I'm your basketball coach this year. My name is Coach Acevedo."

Coach Acevedo?

"This year's fifth-grade basketball program is going to be a little bit different. Make that, this year's fifth-grade basketball program is going to be a lot bit different."

"Where's Coach Lebo?" a girl asked.

"Coach Lebo is only coaching the varsity team this year.

I'm running the fifth-grade program, and as you can see, it's no longer just for RJE students." He drew a circle in the air with his finger. "The basketball programs have been consolidated this year, and if you don't know what *consolidated* means, look it up when you get home."

I'm pretty sure I knew what *consolidated* meant. It's like when you try stuffing all your socks, T-shirts, and underwear into the same drawer.

I checked Red. He stood on my left, his eyes fixed on Coach Acevedo like back in class.

"The basketball program is now a district program, and because it's a district program, not everyone can make the team."

"Make the team?" the same girl said.

"Make the team," Coach Acevedo said. "There's only room for twelve or thirteen of you."

"So are we having tryouts or something?" Jordan asked.

"We are. An hour of tryouts today and an hour of tryouts on Saturday. Our first official practice is Tuesday. Two weeks from Saturday, we have our first game."

Game.

Two weeks from Saturday, we have our first game.

You know that feeling you get when you're supposed to go to the beach for the weekend, and your mom cancels the trip the day before because she has to work? Or the feeling you get when you're finally first in line for Nitro, and you're not allowed on because you don't meet the crappy height requirement? Or that feeling you get when you catch the puking-your-brains-out stomach bug the day before Xander McDonald's paintball party?

The feeling I had right now felt like all of those wrapped in one.

I checked Red. He was smiling his basketball smile—the mega-grin he gets when he plays ball—and doing his hopping-from-foot-to-foot, I'm-so-excited-I-just-can't-hide-it dance.

I grabbed the back of my neck and squeezed.

He had no idea.

Not. At. All.

Suzanne, his mom, wasn't going to let him play. The fifth-grade basketball program was only supposed to be drills and conditioning. Not games. She didn't think Red was ready for *real* basketball.

He wasn't ready for real basketball. He wasn't going to let an opposing player—someone he didn't know—body him up.

He'd freak.

I brushed the locks off my forehead. We weren't going to be able to play basketball together.

"The league we're playing in is not a school league,"

Coach Acevedo continued. "We'll be playing against teams from all over the county."

"Is it co-ed?" another girl asked.

"It is," Coach Acevedo said, "but not every team will have boys and girls on their roster. Some of the teams . . . well, we'll get to that later. Our team will have boys and girls on the roster."

Tweet! Tweet!

"Enough with all this talking," he said. "Let's get poppin'!"

Hoops Madness

The forty-eight fifth graders in the RJE school gym were not going to be mistaken for the Celtics or the Heat.

Not in a gazillion years.

Tweet! Tweet!

"We don't run with the basketball!" Coach Acevedo said over and over during the first ball-handling drill. "That's called traveling. When we run with the ball, we lose possession of the ball."

Tweet! Tweet!

"We don't dribble the basketball with two hands," he said over and over during the next ball-handling drill. "We dribble with one hand. When we dribble with two, we lose possession of the ball."

Nah, I wasn't running with the basketball or dribbling with two hands, but I wasn't in basketball mode either, and when I'm on the court, I'm *always* in basketball mode.

What's basketball mode? When I'm playing ball, I'm

all about hoops. *All* about hoops. My brain focuses on nothing else.

Which is how it should be.

But not today.

Today, I couldn't shake Red from my head. We were finally on a basketball court together at RJE. We were lining up next to each other for every drill. But all I could think about was what was going to happen later.

That's not to say I wasn't having fun. Of course I was having fun. I was playing ball, how could I not be having fun? But I was distracted, and I'm never distracted on the basketball court.

So I started doing play-by-play for Red. That helped.

"Red dribbles down the right side," I announced. "He circles past the first cone, switches to his left, and heads for midcourt. Look at the way this kid handles the rock. He nears the timeline and . . . oh, what a great-looking crossover!"

A Free-Throw-Shooting Machine!

At the foul line, Red trapped the ball soccer-style under his left foot. He placed a finger over each earplug and took several breaths. Then with both hands, he picked up the ball, squared his shoulders, and looked at the front rim. He dribbled three times low to the ground—hard dribbles—and then stood back up. He spun the ball until his fingers were around the word SPALDING. He looked at the rim again, extended his arms, and took the shot.

Underhanded.

Swish.

"Boo-yah!" I shouted. "Twelve!"

I scooped up the ball, dribbled it back, and put it on the line next to Red. Then we went right into our handshake: "High-five, high-five. Elbow, elbow," we said together. "Right, right, left, left, fist, fist, knuckles, blow it up. Turn, jump, bump . . . boo-yah!"

We'd started doing the handshake after Red hit his seventh in a row.

At the end of practice, Coach Acevedo wanted everyone taking foul shots until we got picked up. Red and I shot with the group at the hoop by the stage, but since we walked home and could stay the latest, we went last.

At the line, Red went through his routine and took his next underhanded free throw.

Swish.

"Thirteen!" I leaped. "Unstoppable!"

I grabbed the rebound, we danced through our handshake, and Rip went back to work.

"What a performance Red is putting on," I play-by-played. "Do I hear fourteen?"

Swish.

"Fourteen!" I hammer-fisted the air.

"Blake Daniels can't miss." He popped his Warriors logo. "Blake Daniels is on fire."

"He sure is!" Coach Acevedo clapped, walking up.

Red turned. His fists shot to his cheeks.

"I've been watching you the whole time," Coach Acevedo said. "You're a free-throw-shooting machine!"

"No one's better than Red from the line," I said.

"That's what I've heard."

"You have, Mr. Acevedo?" Red hunched his shoulders and squinched his nose. "I mean, Coach Acevedo." His fists tapped his cheeks.

"I have." Coach Acevedo turned to me. "You said Rip's a basketball nickname. Like Rip Hamilton from the Detroit Pistons?"

"You've heard of him?"

"Absolutely," Coach Acevedo said. "Excellent team player. Always hustling. Made everyone around him better."

You know when you're playing ball and there's always that one kid who's running around in warp speed? Well, that's me. That's why I'm Rip. Like the guard on the Pistons who never stopped moving. He was also known as the Running Man and wore number thirty-two.

I'm number thirty-two.

I have another nickname: Gnat. Teams called me that the year I played on the third-grade select team because when I play defense, I can be annoying. Really annoying. I'm the kid who picks off the lazy inbounds pass and the kid who sneaks up on the big man posting up down low and strips him from behind.

I love it when teams call me Gnat.

Red set himself on the line and went through his routine.

Swish!

"Fifteen!"

Coach Acevedo grabbed the rebound.

"Listen, Red," he said, walking the ball back to the line. "I know you're not allowed to play in games. Your mom and I had a long conversation earlier in the week."

"You did, Coach Acevedo?" He pinky-thumbed his thigh.

"We did. The hospital where she's a nurse is right near my apartment. I met her after work."

I gripped the back of my neck. This was it. This was the moment. I had no idea how Red was going to react.

"I want you on our team, Red." Coach Acevedo glanced at me and then flipped the ball to Red. "You show up for practices, I'll make sure you're *both* on our team."

"I'll show up for practices!" Red dropped the basketball and hugged Coach Acevedo.

I'd never seen Red hug someone he just met.

"I'll show up for practices!" he repeated. "Did you hear that, Mason Irving?"

I hammer-fisted the air.

Lesley Irving

"Knock, knock."

I looked up from my book. "Hey, Mom," I said, pulling out my earbuds.

"Dinner's almost ready," she said, walking into my room. She pushed aside my stuffed animals and sat down next to me on the bed. "How did it go today?"

"It was a day."

"I had a feeling you might say something like that." She tilted my book so she could see the cover. "I adore Sharon Draper. Melody's such a beautiful character."

I was reading *Out of My Mind*. I read all the time, but I'm a slow-mo reader. It takes me forever to finish a book. Even books I love.

"Did you know about Ms. Hamburger?" I asked.

"Yes." She picked lint out of my hair. "We need to relock these. Maybe this weekend."

I ducked away. "Maybe."

"You're not moisturizing enough, Rip. Your scalp is dry."

"You knew I had a new teacher?"

"Yes. What's his name again?"

"Mr. Acevedo. Wait, you knew it was a guy? Why didn't you say something?"

"I didn't want to ruin the surprise. Having a male teacher is going to be good for you this year."

I turned down a corner and closed the book. "He has long hair, piercings, and tattoos."

"Does that matter?"

"I'm just saying." I shrugged. "Did you know about Coach Lebo?"

She leaned against the wall. "Yes, I knew about Coach Lebo and about the new teacher taking over the basketball program."

"It's a league now," I said. "We're playing games against . . . you know all this, don't you?"

"Yes."

"I can't believe you didn't say anything."

"I'm not holding your hand this year, Rip. I said that to you all summer."

"I heard you."

"Did you?"

" 'Life is about playing the cards you're dealt.' " I tossed the book onto the table by my bed. "You said that a gazillion times."

"Glad you listened." She patted my leg.

"How many times did you say that to your students today?"

She laughed. "You have no idea!"

My mom is the principal at River West, a public middle school about twenty minutes away. She started the school a few years ago with some educator friends.

"How did Red do today?" she asked.

"I think okay."

"You think?"

I shrugged. "He did fine."

"I'm sure he was happy you were there."

"Suzanne spoke to the new teacher about . . . you know that, too."

"Yes."

I smacked the bed. "I can't believe you didn't say anything. I was buggin' at practice."

"The new teacher has been so accommodating. Suzanne's so relieved. It would've been awful if—"

"I didn't think Red was going to be allowed to play. It was all I could think about at basketball."

She flicked lint from the locks by my ear. "Are you excited about the new league?"

"We'll be lucky to win a game."

"How can you say that? You haven't even seen the other teams yet."

"Don't need to." I grabbed the Nerf ball from under my purple teddy bear. "Everything's so different with fifth grade. Nothing's what I expected."

"Honey, I tried to tell you this over the summer."

"I know."

"Once the voters rejected the budget and bond initiative back in the spring, I knew we were in for it." She shook her head. "People didn't understand what they were voting for. The cuts I have to make . . . It's awful. Everyone's going to see this damage." She bumped my shoulder. "Hey, fifth grader, why are all your clothes on the floor?"

I shot the Nerf at the hoop above my closet. It bounced off the front rim. "I always leave my clothes on the floor."

She pinched her thumb and index finger together. "I just thought there was a teeny-tiny chance things might be different this year."

"I'll work on it."

"Work a little harder." She swatted my leg and stood up. "I'm not entertaining the thought of a dog around here until you learn to pick up after yourself."

"I'm learning."

"Come downstairs in ten for dinner."

"Text me."

"Text you?" She shot me a look. "And you wonder why you don't have a phone yet?"

"Just playin'."

"You'd better be, Mason Irving."

Community Circle

"**Let's have a conversation,**" Mr. Acevedo said after attendance the next morning. "Come join me in the meeting area."

In Room 208, the meeting area was on the left when you walked in. A blue carpet began by the door and went all the way to the cubbies in the back. There was a denim sofa, six green polka-dotted beanbag chairs, and a bathtub. Yeah, a bathtub, one of those old-fashioned ones with feet. A cardboard sign propped against it read: ONE FIFTH GRADER AT A TIME.

The kids sitting at the tables closest to the carpet grabbed the beanbag chairs, and since Mariam was first to the sofa, she saved spots for Olivia and Grace. Zachary snagged the bathtub.

"You don't need your chair," Mr. Acevedo said to Red. "Leave it at your table."

Red stopped.

Red doesn't like sitting on the floor. He only sits on the floor in his bedroom and in my basement. He was bringing his chair because there weren't any seats left.

He turned to me and squinched his nose and forehead. Old-man face.

I checked the couch and beanbags. If Ms. Yvonne were here, she would've asked someone to get up. But I couldn't, because if I did and no one got up, I had no idea how Red would react.

"It'll be fine, Red," I said. "It's only for a few minutes."

He hunched his shoulders and tightened his grip on the chair.

"It's only for a few minutes," I said again, hopefully.

He still didn't move.

"A few minutes, Red." I placed my hand next to his on the chair. "Just for a few minutes."

Slowly, he loosened his fingers. When his hands were back by his sides, I returned the chair to our table. Then we made our way to the carpet and sat down by the door.

Red sat with his knees to his chest and his arms wrapped around his legs.

"Where would you like to sit, Ms. Goodman?" Mr. Acevedo asked Avery.

Ms. Goodman.

Yesterday, when Mr. Acevedo asked Avery what she wanted to be called, she said Ms. Goodman.

She pointed across the carpet.

"Let's make some room." Mr. Acevedo motioned for everyone to clear a path.

"Dude, move," she growled at me.

Avery had plenty of room to get by. But I knew better than to say anything.

Everyone does.

I looked away and checked the room.

There were already a whole bunch of charts up on the front wall. They all said WRITING TIPS across the top, but only one had something written on it.

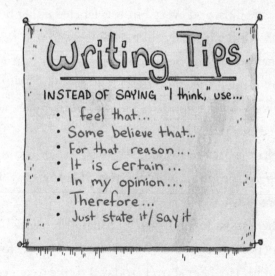

Writing Tips

INSTEAD OF SAYING "I think," use...
- I feel that...
- Some believe that...
- For that reason...
- It is certain...
- In my opinion...
- Therefore...
- Just state it/say it

In the back above the cubbies, a large sign said CONFUSING WORDS AND HOMOPHONES. There were already a few listed—pier/peer, your/you're, aloud/allowed, fir/fur. The definitions were underneath each. Most of the back wall was going to be covered in confusing words and homophones.

The corner by the windows was the Swag Corner. It said SWAG CORNER in big blue graffiti letters. One of the teachers at my mom's school has a Swag Wall in her class. It's where she puts up the best work.

In the other back corner, written in the same graffiti font, were the words YO! READ THIS! There was a scan of a book cover and beneath it, a plot summary and review. Book recommendations were going to go there.

Books were everywhere in Room 208. Most were in clear plastic bins, and every bin was labeled either by author or genre. No lie, it looked like Mr. Acevedo had raided the Container Store! The only books not in clear bins were the ones on top of the cubbies. They were in all different containers—silver toolboxes, colored milk crates, and old-fashioned metal lunchboxes.

"Welcome back to Room 208," Mr. Acevedo said. He sat cross-legged on the floor between Danny and Hunter. "Welcome to—"

"Where's Ms. Hamburger?" Declan interrupted.

"Patience, grasshopper," Mr. Acevedo said. He folded his hands in his lap. "For starters today, I'd like to tell everyone a little about myself: *Yo soy dominicano, y toda mi familia también. Mi familia es de Santiago, una ciudad situada en el centro de la República Dominicano."* He paused. *"Levanten sus manos aquellos que pueden hablar español."*

Bryan, Diego, Zachary, Christine, and Isa raised their hands.

"Bueno," Mr. Acevedo said. He drummed his legs. "I'm Dominican. My family is from Santiago, a town in the middle of the island of Santo Domingo. That's what I just said. Then I said, if you know Spanish, raise your hand."

"I also speak Italian, Mr. A.," Zachary said.

"We speak Russian," Lana said, pointing to her twin sister, Ana. "Not as well as everyone in our family, but we understand it."

"Excellent," Mr. Acevedo said. "For those of you who can speak a second language, keep on learning it. Learn to read it, write it, master it. For those of you who don't know a second language, learn one. It's never too late to start. My girlfriend just started learning Arabic."

I checked Mr. Acevedo. He wore the same jeans as yesterday, just like he said he would, but today he wore a T-shirt, a red one with an equal sign across the front. Since he was wearing short sleeves, everyone could see his tats. I tried reading the quote on his arm, but it wrapped all the way around, so I could only make out some of the words. Something about a ship.

"Welcome to Community Circle—CC," Mr. Acevedo

said. "That's what we're calling this." He drew a circle in the air with his finger. "A few times each week, we're coming together and having conversations. Sometimes they'll last two minutes, sometimes they'll last twenty, and sometimes they may last the whole period."

"What are we going to talk about?" Attie asked.

"All different things. We'll have conversations about school, we'll have conversations about current events, we'll have conversations about books. We'll definitely have conversations about books."

I checked Red. He still had his arms around his legs. His eyes were fixed on Mr. Acevedo.

"Now who can tell me what was the last thing I said yesterday?" Mr. Acevedo asked.

Red's hand shot up. Mr. Acevedo pointed to him with his chin.

" 'Tune in tomorrow for another exciting episode of *Room 208, Unexpected.*' " Red grinned. "That was the last thing you said yesterday, Mr. Acevedo."

"It sure was, Red." Mr. Acevedo laughed. "What about the sentences before that?" He nodded to Miles.

"We have to bring something to read to class every day."

"Exactly. We have independent reading every day in Room 208, every single day. We're calling it Choice. We can read whatever we want: books, poetry, comics, graphic novels, magazines, e-books. So long as you're reading. I know I'll be reading. I'll be wearing my sign, too." He pointed to the do-not-disturb sign on the back of his chair. "Feel free to make your own signs."

"How long will we have for Choice?" Melissa asked.

"It depends. Some days maybe ten or fifteen minutes, some days an hour."

"Can we listen to audiobooks?" she asked.

"Absolutely," he replied. "Reading with our ears is definitely permitted." He brushed the hair out of his eyes. "So we have Choice in here every day, and I'll be reading to you in here every day."

"Does that have a special name, too, Mr. A.?" Danny asked, smiling.

"As a matter of fact, it does, Danny." Mr. Acevedo smiled back. "We're calling it Teacher's Theater Time—T3." He pointed his index fingers at Declan. "Now it's time for those answers, answers, answers. Ask me your question."

"Where's Ms. Hamburger?"

"She retired. A lot of teachers did."

Red wrapped his arms around his legs again and swayed. I placed my hand on his back.

"Why did everyone retire?" Declan followed up.

"Money." Mr. Acevedo rubbed his thumb against two fingers. "Money is super tight. That's why I'm here. We new teachers are getting paid a whole lot less to do a whole lot more. I'm teaching fifth-grade Language Arts, fourth-grade science, third-grade—"

"Fourth grade?" Isa said. "Ms. Wright retired, too?"

"She did," Mr. Acevedo said. "I'm teaching three different grades here, driver's ed two afternoons a week up at the high school, and—"

"How can one person do all that?" I interrupted.

Mr. Acevedo laughed. "I've been asking myself the same question, Rip."

Red swayed faster. He turtled his neck, too.

"Is Ms. Darling still the principal?" Isa asked.

"She is." Mr. Acevedo nodded. "But she's going to be out of the building a lot the first few weeks. That's why you haven't seen her these first two mornings. They've cut almost all the assistant-principal positions in the district, so all the principals are trying to figure out—"

"Wait a sec," Declan said. "The principal's out of the building, and there's no AP. So who's in charge?"

Mr. Acevedo patted his chest. "That would be me, the brand-new teacher who's not afraid to shake things up."

"You're in charge of the whole school?" Piper asked.

"Not exactly," Mr. Acevedo said. "But I am in charge in here. That means I'm teaching this class the way I want. That means we're going to have fun in here." He chuckled. "Of course, it may also mean I'm a delusional rookie teacher, and if you don't know what *delusional* means, look it up."

I had no idea what *delusional* meant. It sounded like something contagious or deadly.

"I'm only here for a year," Mr. Acevedo said. "I have a one-year contract. So I'm looking at this as an opportunity— an opportunity for everyone." Mr. Acevedo drummed his legs again. "Now let's get poppin'. Time for our first T3."

Teacher's Theater Time

With my basketball eyes, I followed Mr. Acevedo as he walked the classroom while reading *Lawn Boy* by Gary Paulsen. It's an awesome story about this kid who gets a beat-up old mower from his grandmother for his birthday. Then he goes into business with his crazy but super-smart neighbor named Arnold. Before he knows it, he's making loads of dough.

At RJE, all the teachers read to their classes, but I'd never had a teacher read like this. It didn't feel like Mr. Acevedo was reading. It felt like the boy—the narrator—was reading. For the different characters, like the grandmother and Arnold, Mr. Acevedo used different voices. Sometimes he read quickly, sometimes slowly. His voice rose and fell as he strutted, dipped, slid, and danced around the tables. He stood on the tables, too. And when Mr. Acevedo stopped to ask a question about a character or to have us make a prediction, he did it in such a way that it didn't interrupt the flow. It was almost as if that was part of the performance, too.

Yeah, it was a performance. Like being at a theater.

Teacher's Theater Time.

"That's all, folks," he said, closing the book just before the end of a scene. "Tune in tomorrow for another exciting episode of *Room 208, Unexpected*."

Up

Twenty-two hours and thirty minutes later . . .

"Here are your instructions," Mr. Acevedo said, hopping onto his desk. "I want everyone to get a journal." He pointed to the composition notebooks on the windowsill behind Red and me. "Put your name on it, and then go stand on your table."

Go stand on your table.

Red raised his fists to his face and tapped his cheeks.

"Just be careful," Mr. Acevedo said. "I don't want to have to write an incident report on my third day." He jumped down and scooted to Avery. "What can you do, Ms. Goodman?"

She curled her lip. "Well, I can't exactly stand on my table."

"I didn't think you could." He tapped her armrest. "But you're a member of this class, and everyone in Room 208 participates. So what can we have you do instead?"

"Whatever," she said.

"Nope." Mr. Acevedo shook his head. "We need to come up—"

"I can climb," she interrupted.

"Excellent. Be right back." He slide-stepped to the door and leaned into the hallway. "Ms. Waldon," he called, "can you send one of the custodians our way?"

Ms. Waldon, the parent coordinator.

She hadn't been at her desk these first three mornings, and I was afraid to ask where she was. Ms. Waldon knew everything about RJE. *Everything.* Mom called people like Ms. Waldon indispensable.

I pushed my chair away from the table, reached back, and grabbed two notebooks. I placed one in front of Red, who still had his hands by his face. He was swaying, too.

Whenever we had writer's workshop or a new writing assignment in ELA, Red always worked with Ms. Yvonne.

I wrote RIP in all caps on the cover of my notebook and then tapped Red on the shoulder. "Come on," I said, standing up. "This could be fun."

He continued to sway.

I shook out my hair. I was pretty sure Red would be fine once he was up. Everyone was doing the assignment, too. It wasn't like he was being singled out.

"Come on," I said again.

"Okay, Mason Irving," he said softly.

We both climbed onto our table.

"Freeze!" Mr. Acevedo suddenly shouted.

Everyone froze.

"Without moving your feet," he said, "turn and look my way." Mr. Acevedo stood in the doorway with his arm around Mr. Goldberg.

Mr. Goldberg, the head custodian.

"If you don't know who this man is," Mr. Acevedo said, "you need to learn. This is Mr. Goldberg. After the twenty-six of you in Room 208, this gentleman right here is the most important person in the school. Not only does he know where everything is, he also has the key to every door. That means, he has access. That means, we're always kind to this man."

Mom called people like Mr. Goldberg indispensable, too.

"We're doing a writing activity." Mr. Acevedo turned to him. "Would it be possible to borrow a stepladder?"

"Coming right up." Mr. Goldberg ducked into the hallway.

"Can we unfreeze?" Trinity asked. She was standing with one foot on her chair and one foot on her table.

"Not until the ladder arrives," Mr. Acevedo said.

It arrived a few moments later.

"Here you go, Ms. Goodman," Mr. Acevedo said, opening it next to her. "Do you need help getting—"

Avery was already lifting herself out of her chair. She began pulling herself up the ladder.

I'd never seen Avery out of her chair. I'm pretty sure most of the other kids hadn't either.

Everyone stared.

"What are you looking at?" she said when she reached the top rung.

Mr. Acevedo handed Avery her journal and then sprang onto his desk. "This activity is about perspective," he said. "Room 208 looks very different from up here. We're looking at things from a new vantage point, a new point of view. That enables us to see the things we always see in a different way. It also allows us to discover new things right in front of us. I want you to write down what you see. How do things look different from up here? What new things have appeared?"

"Can we draw?" Sebi asked.

"Absolutely," Mr. Acevedo answered. "Draw, write, whatever, and for this exercise, don't worry about full sentences, capital letters, or spelling. Just get your ideas and observations down on the page. Use your senses. What do you see? What do you hear? What do you feel? Give me details. Lots of specific details. Details make our writing come to life."

It sounded pretty cool. And I loved that he said don't worry about full sentences, capital letters, or spelling!

I did my best:

Rip   Thursday, September 5

STANDING ON TABLE ASSIGNMENT

The light bulbs are humming

There's a dead wasp in the ficture,
I can see it's legs.

The top of the ficture has never been
dusted.

The top of the cieling projector has
never been dusted

It's hot up here

Red isn't writing

Mr. Acevedo has a tattoo on the back
of his neck.

A ship is safe in harbor, but that's not
what ships are for. That's what his
tattoo on his arm says.

Out the window. the tops of the
portables.

Out the window. the soccer field on
the other side of the portables.

Out the window, part of the fence
around the playground

Red still isn't writing

At first I was nervous standing up
here. Now I'm not.

The T-Word

Twenty-two hours and fifteen minutes later...

"We survived the first week!" Mr. Acevedo said, raising both arms. "Yeah, it was only a four-day week, but we made it. Next week we're here Monday to Friday. That's our first real test." He gasped. "Test? Test!"

Suddenly, he clutched his chest and stumbled forward like a person pretending to have a heart attack on an old television show. He staggered across the carpet, fell onto a beanbag, and rolled next to the bathtub.

Then he bounced to his feet.

"That Oscar-worthy performance was brought to you by the T-word." He formed the letter *T* with his hands. "*Test* is the T-word. Just like we're not permitted to use the H-word at RJE, we're not permitted to use the T-word in Room 208." He spun to Attie, whose hand was up.

"But we have to take—"

"Don't say it!" He cut her off. "Don't say the T-word.

Now I'm about to use it because I want to explain myself, but once I do, we're not wasting our time discussing tests and testing in Room 208."

He walked past our table to the front closet.

"You see these?" He opened the door. The closet was filled with test prep booklets. Like the ones from last year. And the year before. "These will not be seeing the light of day in here." He shut the door. "I'm not about tests and test scores." He motioned to Attie, whose hand was back up.

"But we still have to take . . . assessments."

"We do."

"Then how will we—"

"You'll do fantastic. Everyone will."

"But what if we don't?" Attie said.

I was thinking the same things. How could we not do test prep? We had even more tests this year than in third and fourth grade. Some counted for middle-school placement. We *needed* to do test prep.

"Attie, if you don't do well," Mr. Acevedo said, "I'm one and done. They give me the boot at the end of the year." He wagged his finger. "But that's not going to happen. You will learn in here. Everyone will learn in here. I guarantee it." He pointed to Diego's raised hand.

"Are you giving us T-words?"

"Good question, Diego." Mr. Acevedo leaned against his

desk. "For the most part, no. I'll be assessing you in other ways. I'm about real assessment that's useful. I'll be giving you feedback, so we understand purpose, because that's how we learn to think." He adjusted a hoop in the top of his ear. "You've only known me three days, but I think you can see I tend to do things a little differently." He bongo-drummed the side of his desk. "Now let's talk about your homework assignment for the weekend."

"I thought you said you don't believe in homework," Jordan said.

"That's not what I said, Jordan. I said I'm not a big fan of homework. And this homework assignment—the purpose of it—is to get everyone thinking about our class project."

"What class project?" several kids asked at once.

"Another good question," Mr. Acevedo said. "The answer to it will be posted on our class webpage this evening." He jumped and smacked the URL written on the blue sentence strip above the board. "It's your responsibility to check this. You're in fifth grade now. I'm not holding your hands."

My forehead fell to the table. Sometimes Mr. Acevedo sounded a little too much like my mom.

H-O-R-S-E

"**We're playing basketball,**" Red sang, rocking in the gaming chair. "We love that basketball."

"You're going down today, Blake Daniels," I said. I was on my stomach lying across the sectional couch.

"We'll see about that, Mason Irving." Red's eyes stayed on the flat screen.

Red and I play Xbox in my basement all the time, but Red can only play a few games, and he's not very good at the games he does play. Except for Horse. That's *his* game, and when Red's locked in, I don't stand a chance.

Red was locked in.

"Magic Johnson was the most valuable player of the NBA three times," he said. He took the one-handed, over-the-shoulder shot from the top of the key. "Bam! Magic Johnson was the most valuable player in 1987, 1989, and 1990. He was also the most valuable player of the NBA finals three times. In 1980, 1982, and 1987."

Whenever we play Horse, we play the "Legends" version. Red's a different legend every time.

"Magic Johnson was an all-star twelve times," he said. "He was the most valuable player of the All-Star Game two times. In 1990 and 1992."

Any guesses who he was today?

I was Allen Iverson. I was always Iverson.

"Irving works the stick," I slow-mo play-by-played, because that's the only way to play-by-play Horse. "He slides Iverson into place, checks the arc, the one-handed, over-the-shoulder shot . . . it's good! Yes! Oh, Irving is matching Daniels hoop-for-hoop this afternoon!"

"I'm still up H-O-R to H-O," Red said. He rocked forward, grabbed his sweet tea off the Rubix Cube table, and took a drink. "Refresh the page," he said. "See if the assignment's up."

"I just checked a minute ago."

"Check again."

I reached for the MacBook on the floor, paused the Let's Play vid, and clicked back to the class page. There it was. The assignment. And to be perfectly honest, it sounded amazing.

"It's up!" I said.

"What's the assignment?" Red dove beside me. "What does it say?"

I read out loud:

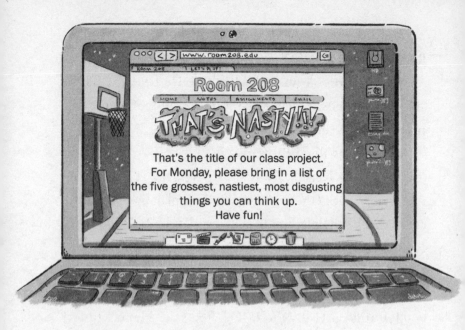

That's the title of our class project.
For Monday, please bring in a list of
the five grossest, nastiest, most disgusting
things you can think up.
Have fun!

"Explosive diarrhea!" I shouted.

"Explosive macaroni and cheese diarrhea!" Red said.

"Oh, nasty!" I clawed my hands against my cheeks. "Explosive macaroni and cheese *and* cotton candy ice cream diarrhea!"

"Cotton candy ice cream puke!"

"Hold on." I minimized the page and pulled up a Sticky. "We need to get these down. *Cotton candy ice cream puke*," I said as I typed. "*Macaroni and cheese diarrhea*. What else?"

"Wait." Red pointed to Magic Johnson. "I haven't finished beating you."

"Beating me?"

"Beating you, Mason Irving." He slid onto his chair.

"You're buggin', Red."

At half-court, Magic held a ball in each hand. He tossed one into the air and as it came down, he punched it into the air with the other. The ball sailed across the court and through the hoop. "Bam!" Red waved his arms. "Take that, Mason Irving!"

"Rotten cucumbers," I said. "Mushy rotten cucumbers growing alien-head white spots."

"Bad chicken." Red stuck out his tongue. "One time, we had bad chicken in the fridge. It stunk up the whole house."

From half-court, Iverson batted the ball toward the hoop. It didn't reach the foul line.

"Bam!" Red bounced. "H-O-R-S for Mason Irving, H-O for Blake Daniels." He grabbed his bare foot. "Stinky feet!"

"Time for my comeback," I said.

"Magic Johnson averaged 11.2 assists per game," Red said, moving Magic around the screen. "In the playoffs, Magic Johnson had 2,346 assists, more than any other player in history."

"Boogers," I said. "Crusty brown-and-green boogers!"

"If you're trying to distract me, it's not working."

"Not washing your hands after doing number two." I grabbed the back of his chair and rocked it.

"Still not working, Mason Irving," Red said. "In 1992, Magic Johnson was an Olympic gold medalist. In 1996, he was named one of the fifty greatest players in NBA history. In 2002, he was elected to the Basketball Hall of Fame."

"Not washing your hands after explosive macaroni and cheese and cotton candy ice cream diarrhea!"

Red took a soccer shot from the parking lot outside the arena.

Swish!

"Bam!" He jumped up. "They're playing basketball," he sang. "We love that basketball."

Clifton United

At the start of the second tryout, Coach Acevedo had us run five laps around the gym.

That didn't go so well.

After the first lap, some kids needed to walk. After the second, some kids had to stop. And after the third, the line for the water fountain in the alcove behind the basket went all the way to the free-throw line.

Red and I ran our five laps with the lead group.

"Some of these kids aren't in very good shape," he said as we waited for everyone to finish.

"Not at all."

I was in full basketball mode today. Red was hopping from foot to foot.

When everyone finished, Coach Acevedo broke us into groups and sent us to the six baskets for shooting drills.

Those didn't go so well either.

Balls flew in every direction—banging off the backboards,

sailing into the cafeteria, ricocheting off the front of the stage—and kids were running into one another trying to chase them down. No lie, at times the gym looked like human bumper cars!

"I don't think some of these kids have played very much basketball before," Red said.

We stood against the mat under our hoop. I had my arm up ready to block anything incoming.

"I *know* some of these kids haven't played very much basketball before," I said.

Tweet! Tweet!

"Before someone gets hurt out here," Coach Acevedo said, jogging to midcourt and waving his arms, "let's line up for some ball-handling drills."

This wasn't going to be pretty either.

I was right.

The first kid dribbled the ball off his foot, and when he ran after it, he tripped over the stack of mini orange cones.

Tweet! Tweet!

"Let's watch where we're going out there," Coach Acevedo said.

The next kid took three steps before putting the ball on the floor.

Tweet! Tweet!

"Like I said on Tuesday," Coach Acevedo said, "we can't run with the ball."

The next kid dribbled with both hands.

Tweet! Tweet!

"Like I said the other day," Coach Acevedo said, "we can't dribble with two hands."

The next kid didn't turn at the first cone. Instead, he kept going straight and dribbled right into the ball rack, knocking all the balls onto the court.

"Like I said," Red whispered, "I don't think some of these kids have played very much basketball before."

"Like I said, I *know* some of these kids haven't played very much basketball before."

* * *

After the last drill, Coach Acevedo huddled us at midcourt.

"Thank you for trying out for Clifton United," he said.

Clifton United.

All the Clifton schools coming together to form one team: Clifton United.

I liked it.

"Now here's how this is going to work." Coach Acevedo twirled his whistle. "To those of you in my class, this will sound a little familiar. Tomorrow evening, I'll be posting the roster on our team webpage. It's your responsibility to check—"

Several hands shot up.

"Hold on." He motioned the hands down. "Yes, Clifton

United has a webpage. When your parents signed you up, one of the questions on the application asked your parents whether they thought you were responsible enough to check the team webpage on your own."

"My mother made me answer that question," said one of the boys.

So did mine. But I didn't say so.

"Clifton United will not be relying on texting as our primary means of communication," Coach Acevedo said. "I know that's how it's done with other teams, but not every fifth grader has a phone. So for us, it's our webpage." He snatched his whistle. "I've already uploaded a bunch of items—the league rules, the taunting guidelines, the head-injury policy, the Code of Conduct contract. Everyone needs to sign that contract before the first game."

Coach Acevedo looked around the huddle. He made eye contact with some of the kids.

"If you're not selected for the team, try not to be too disappointed. There could be any number of reasons why you weren't chosen this time. For some of you, your parents prefer that you play later in the year."

He did the eye-contact thing again. He looked at Red last.

"Everyone in this gym brings value to Clifton United."

Teammates!

The next night, Red and I were back in my basement playing Xbox. This time, Red had the MacBook and was refreshing the team page as often as the Internet would let him.

Yeah, we already knew we'd made the team, but we still wanted to see our names on the roster.

"It's up!" he shouted. He grabbed the laptop, dove off his chair, and slid across the carpet.

I read the screen:

CONGRATULATIONS!

The following individuals have been selected to play for Clifton United, Fall Ball Season I.

I scrolled down.

1. Khalil Ahmed
2. Wilfredo Benítez
3. Blake Daniels

"Bam!" Red kicked the carpet.

4. Mikey Flynn
5. Leslie Holmes
6. Mason Irving

"Boo-yah!" I leaped onto the sofa.

Red jumped next to me. "We're playing basketball," he sang.

"We love that basketball!" we sang, and danced.

That's Nasty!

On Monday morning, Mr. Acevedo started CC with a quote in Spanish.

"No hay peor sordo que aquel que no quiere oír," he said.

Mr. Acevedo sat cross-legged on the rug in the same spot as the other day. I sat in the same spot, too. Red was on the couch between Christine and Zachary because when Xander saw that Red didn't have a seat, he gave up his place.

It was pretty cool seeing Red sit between two people in a classroom.

"That's something *mi abuela* used to say," Mr. Acevedo said. "Any of my Spanish speakers want to take a shot at what it means?"

"Your grandmother used to say that," Bryan said.

"Something about not listening and not being able to hear," Christine added.

"Very close," Mr. Acevedo said, smiling.

"There's no worse person than someone who doesn't want to listen," Zachary said.

"Excellent." Mr. Acevedo gripped his ankles. "Anyone want to take a shot at what that means?" He motioned to Diego.

"People need to listen," Diego said. "If you don't listen, it's worse than not being able to hear."

"Exactly, Diego. We don't listen anymore, and by we, I mean people in general. We talk and yell over one another, but we don't listen."

"What?" Grace said, smiling.

"Yeah, I can't hear you, Teach," Declan added, grinning.

Mr. Acevedo pointed playfully. "Funny stuff, you two."

"Two ears, one mouth," Trinity said, moving her fingers from her ears to her lips. "My dad says God gave us two ears and one mouth, so we should listen twice as much as we speak."

"I like that," Mr. Acevedo said. He grabbed his ankles again and rocked back and forth. "We're all going to become better listeners in here. Listening leads to learning." He nodded to Miles.

"So what is 'That's Nasty'?" Miles asked.

"A perfectly timed question." Mr. Acevedo popped to his feet and turned toward his desk. "Let's head back to our tables. Take out those lists you made over the weekend."

* * *

Mr. Acevedo grabbed the remote from the binder shelf and powered up the ceiling projector.

"Let's hear what you got," he said. "I want to be dazzled and disgusted." He grabbed the green pen. "Throw out—or throw up—the grossest, most offensive, nastiest things you came up with."

"Picking your teeth with your toenails!" Melissa shouted.

"OHHH!"

"I got one," Danny said. "The yellow tiles by the urinals in the boys' bathroom."

"EWWW!"

"Cotton candy ice cream puke!" I said.

"OHHH!"

As everyone called out examples, Mr. Acevedo wrote them down. Fifteen minutes later, the board was covered with the names of all sorts of disgusting stuff, from crusty earwax globs to poop-filled diapers.

"Outstanding work, everyone." Mr. Acevedo patted the board. "I am dazzled and disgusted. This is going to be a brilliant book."

"Book?" at least five or six of us said at the same time.

"That's right," Mr. Acevedo said. "We're writing a book."

THAT'S NASTY!

- Earwax
- Cotton Candy Ice Cream Puke
- Hair in food
- Picking teeth w/ toenails
- Zits!
- Spoiled milk
- Sweat Stains
- Boogers
- Gas station bathrooms
- Stepping in dog poop
- Rotten dog food
- Dirty diapers

He drew a circle in the air with his finger. "That's our class project. We're writing a book together. It's going to be called *That's Nasty!*"

He punched up a presentation on the board.

"Here's an overview of the project," he said. "I'll play it for you in a sec. Everything you need to know about the project is in here—the steps, the rubrics, the conferencing calendar. I've also uploaded this to the webpage." He laser-pointed the wall by the door. "Starting tomorrow, all the project due dates will be posted here."

Several hands shot up.

He air-pressed them down.

"Let me try to answer some of these before I even hear

them," Mr. Acevedo said. "First, yes, you will work with a partner."

Behind my back, Red gave me a pound.

"However," he added, "*I'm* choosing your partner. Check the webpage this evening."

Slammed Again

I blinked hard. This had to be a mistake.

How can you do this to me?

I refreshed the page again.

Again.

What are you thinking, Mr. Acevedo?

I grabbed the locks above my neck.

Fine, you don't want Red and me working together all the time. So then put me with Danny or Zachary or Hunter. You put Red with X.

I shut the laptop, fell back on my bed, and covered my face with a pillow.

How can you do this to me?

My project partner: Avery Goodman.

Avery

"You think I'm happy about this?" Avery asked.

I didn't say anything back.

We were by the entrance to the playground, near where Red and I leave our bags when we run the obstacle course on the way to school.

When we arrived this morning, Mr. Acevedo told us we needed to *interview* our partners. He handed out a sheet with a list of suggested questions.

"I got these questions from a creative writing class I took in college," he explained. "By answering these questions, we were able to get to know our characters better. I'm hoping these same questions will help you get to know your partners better."

Then he took us out to the playground and went into this whole thing about how he chose our partners and why it was important for us to work with other people.

I scanned the handout on top of my journal:

- *What's on your bed?*
- *Where did you go on your favorite vacation?*
- *If you could have a superpower, what would it be?*
- *What is your favorite genre/type of book?*
- *Who is your favorite singer?*
- *What would your parents say is your most annoying habit?*

I checked Avery. Her open notebook was blank.

"You didn't write anything," I said.

"What?"

"When you climbed the ladder the other day." I motioned to her journal. "You didn't write anything."

She slammed it shut. "Why are you looking in my notebook?"

I turned away. Hunter and Attie stood on the balance beam, talking and laughing. Danny and Diego leaned against the climbing wall, talking and laughing. Lana and Noah, Trinity and Melissa, Gavin and Mariam—all sat on the steps in the amphitheater, talking and laughing.

I checked Red. He and Xander were on a bench diagonally down the walkway. Ms. Yvonne was between them with an open folder in her lap. It was the first time Ms. Yvonne had pushed in to ELA this year. Red and Xander were writing on notecards.

All three were smiling.

I shook out my hair. "Did your wheelchair come with those?" I asked.

"Come with what?"

I pointed to the front of her chair. "Those small tires."

"Dude, they're called casters."

One caster was bright blue, the other bright red. Both had three spokes.

"So did it come with those *casters*?" I asked.

"No."

I let out a puff. "We're supposed to answer these questions." I held up the sheet. "We need—"

"I heard the assignment. I'm not deaf."

"No one said you were."

"Dude, I know what I need to know about you." She curled her lip. "You're the black kid with the twists who lives and breathes basketball."

"Shut up."

"No. It's the truth."

"I don't live and breathe basketball," I said. "And just because I'm black—"

"Whatever, dude."

"No, not whatever, Avery." I pointed to my head. "These are not called twists. They're called locks, *dude*."

"Like I care."

"I care."

"You want something to write down?" She motioned to the handout. "Write this: I'm a wheeler."

I didn't.

"I'm a wheeler," she said again.

"I heard you the first time. I'm not deaf."

"But don't you call me that."

"Call you what?"

"A wheeler."

"Why not?"

"Because you don't." She squeezed her brakes. "Dude, face reality. Around here, you're the black kid who plays basketball, Lana and Ana are the Russian twins, X is the Beatles freak, Red is the autistic kid—"

"Don't say anything about Red."

"Whatever." She rolled her eyes. "He's autistic, right?"

I glared. Yeah, Red was on the spectrum, not that I really knew what that meant. Both my mom and Suzanne have tried explaining it to me a gazillion times, but to be perfectly honest, I don't think Lesley, Suzanne, or any other grown-up gets Red like I do.

"Trinity is the girl who runs track," Avery went on, "Noah is the kid who still drools, and Diego is the only kid in the whole friggin' school who gets to wear a hat. Around here, that's who we are."

"You're wrong," I said.

She pointed to her palm. "Mr. Hipster Know-It-All has got you right here."

"No, he doesn't."

"Dude, you breathe his words."

"No."

She imitated the way Mr. Acevedo played with his hair and earrings. " 'We read every day in Room 208,' " she said, mockingly. " 'I read to you every day, I challenge you to write in your journals, I hate testing, we are—' "

"You're wrong, Avery," I said.

"Dude, you're wrong. Mr. Hipster Know-It-All thinks he knows kids better than anyone, but he doesn't. He gives kids way too much credit." She curled her lip. "You're the black kid who lives and breathes basketball. I'm the wheeler. That's who we are. Deal with it."

All Ball

For the rest of the school day, all I could think about was Avery and the project, and let me tell you, the last thing I wanted to think about was Avery and the project. A few times, I almost went to Mr. Acevedo, but I was too mad.

Thankfully, once I stepped into the gym for Clifton United's first official practice, I shifted into basketball mode.

I love that I can do that.

For the next ninety-five minutes, I was all hoops.

* * *

At the start of practice, we got right down to business.

"Real teams play defense and rebound," Coach Acevedo said. "Teams with heart play defense and rebound. So today, it's all about defense. Let's form two lines between the baseline and foul line."

Tweet! Tweet!

Forming those two lines proved a little challenging for Emily, Mikey, Mehdi, Leslie, Khalil, Jason, Jeffrey, Maya, Alex, Wil, Keith, Red, and me. So Coach Acevedo settled for us standing in the general area.

I checked Red. He was hopping from foot to foot and smiling.

"In order to play defense," Coach Acevedo said, "you have to be in the proper defensive position. That's all about getting in your chairs."

"Chairs?" Red looked around. "What chairs?"

"It's an expression, Red," I said.

"Got it. Thanks, Mason Irving."

"On defense," Coach Acevedo said, "you're sitting in a chair: head up, knees bent, feet shoulder-width apart, heels off the ground." He demonstrated the stance. "When I blow my whistle, everyone get in your chairs."

Tweet!

Everyone did.

"Excellent," Coach Acevedo said. "Now we need to learn how to move on defense. That's all about sliding your feet." He slid back and forth while sitting in his chair. "So here's the drill: First whistle, get in your chairs. Second whistle, slide in that direction." He pointed to the windows. "Next whistle, slide that way." He pointed to the cafeteria wall. "Next whistle, reverse direction. And so on. Here we go."

Tweet!

"In your chairs!" Coach Acevedo called.

Tweet!

"To the right! Other right, Khalil. Other right, Alex. Toward the windows."

Tweet!

"To the left. Toward the wall. Stay in your chairs."

Tweet!

"Windows! Don't cross your legs. Slide! Slide!"

Tweet!

"Wall! Heads up, hands up! Heads up, hands up!"

Tweet!

"Careful, Leslie. Watch where you're going."

Tweet!

Leslie wasn't the only one who needed to be careful. Wil

knocked into Jason, who bowled over Maya and Mehdi. Then Emily stumbled into Jeffrey, who tackled Keith.

That's pretty much how it went for all the drills—running in the wrong direction, tripping over one another, and knocking into things. During full-court pivots and slides—the zigzag drill that no one could figure out—the orange cones were like booby traps. First, Mikey stumbled *twice* before reaching the first cone. Then Alex slid straight up the sideline instead of toward the cone at the top of the key. Then Emily knocked over the first cone *and* the second cone.

"This doesn't look like proper defense," Red said, cupping his hand over his mouth.

"This doesn't look like basketball."

I shook my head.

* * *

"Good job today," Coach Acevedo said at the end of practice. "I like what I saw."

Good job? You liked what you saw?

"Everyone gave it their all today." He twirled his whistle. "That's what I want to see. We played with heart."

"Teams with heart play defense and rebound," Red said, smiling. "Real teams play defense and rebound."

"Exactly." Coach Acevedo gave him a pound. "Once the

season starts, we're not going to have a lot of practice time, so it's important we focus on the foundations now. Our next practice will be all about rebounding." He snatched the whistle. "Now I'm not going to sugarcoat things. Some of the teams we face this season—like Edgemont and Millwood—are pretty stacked, and we have to play Millwood twice. But if we play with heart and we play as a team, we will win this season. I guarantee it."

Soup's On

After school the next day, while I was getting my butt kicked at Horse, all Red wanted to talk about was the project.

"Hairy, smelly, bacteria armpits!" He laughed. "My topic is armpits. How cool is that, Mason Irving? Hairy, smelly—"

"Quit trying to make me miss," I said.

I took the behind-the-back bounce shot from the corner. Air ball.

"That's H-O-R-S to H-O." He rolled off his chair onto his back. "Time to finish you off, Mason Irving. Hairy, smelly, bacteria armpits!"

Lying upside down, he swished an under-the-leg, three-quarter-court shot.

"Bam!" He kicked his feet. "Blake Daniels is unstoppable!"

"Knock, knock."

I checked the stairs. "Hey, Mom."

"Hey, Rip's Mom."

"Let's go, you two." She rapped the railing. "Soup's on."

"Soup's for dinner?" Red said. "We have barbecue chicken for dinner on Wednesday."

"It's an expression," I said. "It means it's time to eat."

"Got it. Time to eat."

When Red stayed over for dinner on weekdays, Mom always served barbecue chicken, salad (with extra cucumbers and no tomatoes), and chips with guacamole.

"We're almost done, Mom," I said. "Give us like—"

"Dinner's on the table," she said. "You're done now."

"I'm ahead H-O-R-S to H-O." Red hit Quit. "I win."

Whoever was ahead when it was time to stop was the winner. That was our rule.

"I'm the king of Horse." Red put his controller on the center orange square of the Rubix Cube table and spun it around. "Game over, Mason Irving."

* * *

At dinner, all Red and Mom wanted to talk about was the project.

"How are things going with Avery?" she asked.

"Do you mind?" I said. "I'm eating."

"That's not very nice, Rip."

"She's not nice."

We were sitting on the stools around the island counter. I was closest to the cabinets, Red was on my right, and Mom was across from us.

"I'm working with Xander McDonald," Red said.

"I like that you're working with Avery," Mom said, tapping my plate with her fork. "It's important to work with other people." She turned to Red. "That goes for both of you. You need—"

"Do all you teacher types have a secret society or something?" I interrupted. "You sound exactly like Mr. Acevedo."

"Great minds think alike. Now if only some of the parents would give him a little breathing room."

"The parents don't like Mr. Acevedo?" I said.

"The barbecue chicken is delicious, Rip's Mom," Red said.

"Thank you, Red."

He held up a chip and dipped it. "The guacamole is delicious, too."

"When are you going to start calling me something other than Rip's Mom?"

He swiveled his stool. "You are Rip's mom."

"Yes, I am. But call me Ms. Irving. Or call me Lesley."

"Can *I* call you Lesley?" I asked.

"Not if you know what's good for you."

"Xander McDonald loves the Beatles," Red said. "That's why he always wears Beatles shirts. He keeps comic books under his bed. His favorite comic is *Batman*. His favorite fruits are mango and banana. His favorite—"

I cut him off. "Mr. Acevedo had us interview our partners."

"What did you learn about Avery?" Mom asked.

"That she has a bad attitude."

"Worse than yours?"

"Whatever."

Whatever.

Avery said *whatever.* The last thing I wanted was to sound like Avery.

"Why don't the parents like Mr. Acevedo?" I asked.

"They do like him." Mom tilted her head. "They're just concerned about the lack of test prep." She laughed. "It's gone from one extreme to another. I've already gotten e-mails."

All the parents know my mom's a principal. Whenever an issue or question comes up at RJE, parents hit her up.

"Mr. Acevedo said he's in charge in Room 208," Red said. "Mr. Acevedo said he gets to teach the class his way."

"We'll see how that goes," Mom said. "Some of these parents are . . . some of the parents are objecting to some of his practices." She nodded to Red. "So how's basketball?"

"Real teams play defense and rebound," he answered, swiveling again. "Our first practice was all about defense. We practiced getting in our chairs and sliding and pivoting and talking to one another. Our next practice is all about rebounding."

"Have you two read the rules and policies your coach posted?"

We both nodded.

"What about the Code of Conduct?" she asked. "Did you turn that in?"

"We will tomorrow," I said.

"Our next practice is tomorrow," Red said. "Then we have practice on Wednesday. Then we have our first game a week from Saturday."

"I see you memorized the schedule," Mom said.

"We have three games the first week," Red said. "We play Edgemont on Saturday the twenty-first. That's an away game. We play O'Malley on Tuesday the twenty-fourth. That's a home game. We play Crystal Lake on Thursday the twenty-sixth. That's an away game. Then we have—"

"You really have memorized the schedule." Mom laughed. "I just wish Suzanne and I were able to make one of those games. Our schedules are nuts these next couple weeks."

"That's okay, Rip's Mom. I don't play in the games. I only practice."

"Red, you may not be playing in games, but I know you. I'm sure you're contributing. That's worth coming to see."

Red basketball-smiled. "Thanks, Rip's Mom."

That was the arrangement Suzanne had worked out with Coach Acevedo. Red practiced with the team, got a uniform, and attended the games. But he didn't play in the games.

That was also the reason why no matter how angry and furious I was at Mr. Acevedo for sticking me with Avery, I couldn't stay angry and furious. He saved a spot on Clifton United for Red.

"Do you wear your earplugs at practice?" Mom asked.

Red nodded. "I wear them during practice, but I take them out when I'm shooting free throws. I don't need to wear earplugs when I'm shooting free throws, Rip's Mom."

I turned to Red. "Handshake?"

"Handshake!"

We spun off our stools.

"High-five, high-five. Elbow, elbow." We chanted our moves. "Right, right. Left, left. Fist, fist, knuckles, blow it up. Turn, jump, bump . . . Boo-yah!"

Happy Reading Day!

The next morning, when we walked into Room 208, Mr. Acevedo was reading in the bathtub and wearing his sign.

Without looking up from his book, he pointed to the board.

> **Happy Reading Day!**
> For the first part of class today, we
> have Choice. For the second part of
> class, it's Teacher's Theater Time. We'll
> be finishing <u>Lawn Boy</u>.

For Choice, I was reading *Geeks, Girls, and Secret Identities*. I'd finally finished *Out of My Mind*, which I'd loved. But now I needed something with robots and superpowers, and so far, this book was perfect.

I checked the room. Like always during Choice, the OMG girls sat on the couch. They each wore do-not-disturb signs like Mr. Acevedo, though their signs had a lot more glitter.

My basketball eyes drifted to the due dates by the door. Avery and I were supposed to have our list of five potential topics today. We were supposed to have started the "preliminary research using the rubric posted on the webpage." We were supposed to conference with Mr. Acevedo next week.

So far, we had nothing. Zero. *Nada.*

Avery wanted our topic to be about getting gum stuck in your hair or something like that. Even though it was boring, I was fine with it, but we still needed to come up with four other topics. Avery refused. She only wanted to do things *her* way, and part of our grade was—

"What?" she snarled.

My eyes shot up. I was staring at her chair. I didn't even realize it. I returned to my book.

I didn't need Avery seeing me looking her way.

Crashing the Boards

"Real teams play defense and rebound," Coach Acevedo said at the start of our second practice. "Teams with heart play defense and rebound. Since our first practice was all about defense—"

"Today is all about rebounding!" Red said.

"Exactly." Coach Acevedo pointed his whistle at Red. "Let's get poppin'."

I checked Red. Rebounding involved physical contact. *A lot* of physical contact.

"Rebounding isn't just a skill," Coach Acevedo said. "It's a state of mind. You don't have to be a good basketball player to be a good rebounder. Sure, it helps if you can jump and catch, but rebounding is just as much about knowing where the ball is going and wanting it more than your opponent."

For the first drill, we formed a single line at midcourt. The first person threw the ball up in the air. The next person caught it.

That was it. That was the whole drill. We practiced catching the basketball.

It went pretty well, except when Alex's throw hit a ceiling light, and for a minute the light swung back and forth like a pendulum and looked like it might come crashing down.

The second drill required a little more skill. It was called Taps. I'd done this drill before. So had Red and Keith.

We formed two lines facing the basket just inside the key. The first person in each line threw the ball against the backboard. The next person in each line caught the ball while jumping in the air, and then while still in the air, threw it against the backboard for the next person. The next person did the same—caught the ball in air and threw it against the backboard.

Coach Acevedo wanted us to make it through the line once.

Yeah, right.

Mehdi, the second person in my line, threw the ball *over* the backboard. Emily, the third person in the other line, threw the ball out the side door of the gym.

Tweet! Tweet!

"Let's switch things up," Coach Acevedo said. "Instead of jumping for the ball, just catch it and throw it against the backboard. No more jumping. We'll work our way up to catching the ball in air."

We never did work our way up, but the drill went a lot better this way.

Tweet! Tweet!

The next rebounding drill was a boxing-out drill. But first, Coach Acevedo had to explain what boxing-out was.

"When a shot goes up," he said, "find your man."

"Or woman," Maya said.

"Or woman." Coach Acevedo nodded. "When a shot goes up, don't go after the ball. Find your *person* and block your person's path to the ball. You do this by pivoting around and feeling for the person." He demonstrated the move. "It's like you're sitting in a chair again."

"The same chairs as on defense?" Khalil asked.

"The exact same chairs," Coach Acevedo said.

I checked Red. He was pinky-thumbing both legs and swaying.

"Real teams play defense and rebound," Coach Acevedo said. "It's all connected. Now this next drill is called the circle drill. Let's get poppin'."

I sidestepped to Red. "I think you may want to sit this one out."

Red hunched his shoulders and squinted his eyes. "I don't know, Mason Irving. I don't know."

I grabbed the back of my neck and glanced at Coach Acevedo. He wasn't looking our way, but some of the others were.

"Sit this one out," I said. I touched his arm.

Red flinched. His pinky-thumbing quickened. His elbows pressed his sides. "I don't know, Mason Irving. I've done every drill."

"Watch it a few times and then decide."

I checked the corner. Coach Acevedo was looking right at us.

"Watch it a few times and then decide," I said again.

Slowly, Red relaxed his shoulders. Then he began to nod. "I think I'll watch it a few times and then decide."

I gave him a pound.

Fix-It Friday

"Welcome to our very first Fix-It Friday," Mr.
Acevedo said after CC on Friday. "Fix-It Fridays are all
about editing."

Everyone groaned. I groaned the loudest. I can't stand
editing and revising.

"Hold on," Mr. Acevedo said. "I used to feel the same
way. I used to H-word revising and editing, but I don't anymore. So my goal is to change the way you feel about revising and editing."

I felt Red's bouncing knees.

Mr. Acevedo picked up a manila folder from his desk
and removed a stack of paper. "Back when I was in school—"

"Was that during the Jurassic Period, Teach?" Declan
called out.

Mr. Acevedo smiled. "Nice one, Declan. As your reward,
why don't you distribute these?" He put the papers in front
of him.

Here's what Declan handed out:

Friday, December, 12

Dear, Parents, Students and Familys:
 We are all deepily saddened by the recent news out of the Domenican Republic. Tropical storm Odette cause millions of dollars in damages and destroyed thousands of homes. Because the storm struck just before the holiday season makes it even more troubling.
 In order to help those familys in need we will be holding and food and clothing drive. Please bring caned goods and clothing to the school cafateria on Monday December, 15.
 Thank you for your supprot and happy holidays.

Sincerly,
Riley Wilson
Principal

I checked Red. He was hunched forward and pinky-thumbing both thighs. I looked at the door, hoping Ms. Yvonne would suddenly appear, even though I knew she wouldn't.

"You okay?" I whispered.

He squinted his eyes.

I put my hand on his knee.

"Back when I was in school," Mr. Acevedo said, "a tropical storm struck the Dominican Republic, Tropical Storm Odette. My school had a large Dominican population, so the principal organized a food and clothing drive and sent out a letter to the community."

"Is this the letter, Mr. A.?" Danny asked.

"It is." Mr. Acevedo waved the paper. "Now this principal wasn't the best writer. I don't fault that. Not everyone writes well. But I do fault not editing and checking over your work. There's no excuse for that. When your name goes on something, you review it. The letter the principal sent out to the community was littered with errors. So you know what my teacher did?"

"She corrected it," Grace said.

"Close. She had us correct it, the class. In fact, she had us correct all of the principal's letters that year. So for this first Fix-It-Friday assignment, you're editing the Tropical Storm Odette letter. You're doing the same assignment I did."

"Can we work with someone?" Attie asked.

"You can work with a partner if you like."

I took my hand off Red's knee and held out my fist.

He gave it a pound.

Full-Court Press

I was at the kitchen counter watching a video when Mom came home, but since I was plugged in, I didn't hear her, so when she touched my shoulder, I jumped and nearly knocked over the water bottle I got at Attie's older brother's bar mitzvah last spring.

"Nice catch," she said.

I flicked out my earbuds. "You scared me."

"I see that." She placed the groceries on the counter by the sink. "Do you think you can put some clothes on?"

I was only wearing my boxers. "Why?"

"Because I said so, that's why. I don't need to give you a reason."

"But there's no one else here."

"I'm here." She opened the fridge and loaded the vegetables into the bottom drawer. "You know I don't like it when you walk around the house in your underwear."

Mom's always telling me to put clothes on around the

house. Just like she's always telling me to pick up the clothes from my bedroom floor. Just like she's always telling me not to dribble in the kitchen. Just like . . .

"What are you watching?" she asked.

I wrapped my ankle around the footrest and swiveled toward her. "These wheelchair basketball guys."

"A wheelchair team played an exhibition here last year."

"Clifton High?"

"No, my school. That's one tough sport." She pointed the celery at me. "Mr. Acevedo posted some items about the project. Have you checked the page?"

"We went over it in class." I shut the laptop.

"I love how organized he is."

"I know you do, Mom."

"Rubrics, checklists, reflection questions, due dates," she said. "It's wonderful. If only some of the parents would back off."

"They're still complaining about Mr. Acevedo?"

"The man's been a teacher for less than a month. Everyone's so quick to hit the testing panic button."

I swiveled back and forth. "We haven't done any test prep."

"So I've been informed. A number of times. Some of the parents want me to say something, but if I say something, it's not going to be what they want me to say." She closed the fridge. "You and Avery are on top of everything?"

"I hope so." I spun off the stool and grabbed an apple from the bag next to the sink.

"Rinse that off before—"

I took a bite.

"Never mind." She reached over and picked a piece of lint from my hair. "We're still on for tomorrow night?"

I nodded.

Mom was re-locking my hair tomorrow night. We were going to watch a movie while she did.

"Have you and Avery decided on your topic?"

"We're working on it."

"Don't take too much longer. You have your conference on Tuesday."

I hopped back onto my stool and swiveled around. "I know."

"I was reading through the conference expectations. There are several steps you need to complete. This project is really about process. You do know that."

"Yes, I know, Mom."

"You don't want to fall behind on something like this, Rip."

"I know."

She placed the grocery bags in the reusables drawer. "You want my advice?"

"You're going to give it anyway, right?"

"Yes, I am." She walked over. "I think you should extend an olive branch."

"What does that mean?" I took another bite.

"It means do something nice."

"She doesn't deserve it."

"Honey, it's not a question of whether she deserves it or not. You two need to figure out a way to work together." She sat down across from me. "One of you needs to make the first move."

"Why does it have to be me?"

"Honey, it's about picking your battles. It's something I tell my students *and* my teachers all the time."

I took another bite, slid off the stool, and faced the compost. "For the win." I lined up the apple.

"Please don't."

I took the shot anyway. It landed in the middle of the bin.

"Boo-yah." I crow-hopped back onto my stool.

"Honey, I want you to try with Avery."

"I am."

"Make the extra effort. Like you do with Red."

"What does Red have to do with this?"

"You don't think you help bring out the best in him?"

"We are who we are. That's what you always say to me."

"Yes, we most certainly are, and Red's an amazing kid with or without you. But there's no denying you help bring out the best in him. You don't think that has something to do with why Mr. Acevedo has you working with Avery?"

"No."

Mom smiled her knowing smile. "Okay."

"It's different with Red," I said.

"You gave him a chance before anyone else did."

"What choice did I have? You and Suzanne are like sisters."

"Neither one of us has forced you to stay friends." She fingered my hair. "Are you having regrets?"

"No." I ducked away.

"Your locks are so ratty."

"Red's my best friend," I said. "Avery's just—"

"Honey, you help bring out the best in Red. Help bring out the best in Avery." She squeezed my fingers. "That's just my two cents. Take it or leave it."

Flat Tires

When my mom gives me her two cents and tells me to take it or leave it, she's really not telling me to take it or leave it.

She's telling me to take it.

Mr. Acevedo's quote at the start of CC on Monday morning didn't exactly help.

"La vida no es esperar a que pase la tormenta . . . es aprender a bailar bajo la lluvia."

"My uncle says that," Diego said.

"Excellent. Do you know what it means?"

"Life isn't about waiting for the storm to pass." He swung his hat strings. "It's about learning to dance in the rain."

"Excellent." Mr. Acevedo strummed his chest. "Let that sink in for a moment."

I didn't need to let it sink in for a moment. I knew what it meant. It was as if my mom had channeled her two cents through some secret educator portal, planted it in Mr. Acevedo's brain, and programmed him to say it.

* * *

"Have you ever gotten a flat tire?" I asked Avery.

"What?" she replied.

"I said, Have you ever gotten a flat tire?"

I sat beside her in Melissa's seat. Melissa was with Trinity on the beanbags, and Declan and Hunter were on Mr. Acevedo's desk, so we had their table to ourselves.

"What do you think?" she said.

"I don't know. I'm asking you."

"Have you ever gotten a flat tire on your bike?"

"Yeah."

"Well then." She rolled her neck.

With my thumb and finger, I pinched a lock above my ear at the root. "We still haven't answered the reflection questions," I said.

"Whatever, dude."

I took the schedule sheet out of my folder. "For the conference, we need to—"

"I said whatever."

I let out a puff. Avery didn't care about the project. She wanted no part of working with me. She wanted no part of being cooperative. She didn't . . .

"First day of school last year," she said softly. "I got a flat the first day last year."

"The first day?"

"The first friggin' day." She squeezed her brakes. "I got thumb-tacked and had to spend the whole morning in the AP's office."

"Ms. Forest's? With the sock puppets?"

Avery nodded.

Ms. Forest had been the assistant principal at RJE up until this year. Her office had shelves and shelves of these creepy sock puppets. Some of them had eyes that seemed to follow you. Whenever Red walked past her office, he always covered his eyes and moved to the far side of the hallway . . . even when her door was closed!

"Those dolls freaked me out," I said.

"Dude, you and me both. I still get nightmares."

We both laughed.

I let out another puff. "So what's the nastiest thing you've ever run over?"

"Huh?" She curled her lip again.

I pointed with my chin to her casters. "What's the grossest, most disgusting thing you've ever run over?" But before she could answer I said, "No, wait. Don't tell me." I held up my hand. "Just think about it."

"Whatever, dude."

"Tell me tomorrow."

Tomorrow

Avery rolled up to my table and opened her journal.

"You wrote them down?" I said, surprised and relieved. I shifted closer. "Can I—"

"Dude!" She yanked away the notebook. "Why are you always looking in my journal? It's called privacy."

I held up my hands and backed away.

She shot me a stare and then slid the notebook onto her lap. "Gas stations are nasty. I never get out of the car at gas stations."

"Why not?"

"Are you going to let me finish?" She curled her lip. "Even if I have to go, I never get out of the car at gas stations because one time when I did, I rolled in gas and oil. Everything stunk forever. The fumes made you want to puke all the time."

"Gas and oil?" I opened my journal. "Can I write this down?"

"Whatever." She turned the page. "Tar is nasty. Tar melts.

Treadmarks

- gas stations: rolling in gas STINKS!

- TAR! (especially in summer)
- rolling over dog poop
- worms on sidewalk after rain

- CHEWING GUM IS THE WORST

- phlegm wads - ran over one this weekend!

- toilet paper - think getting it stuck on your shoe is embarrassing?

- used band-aids - YUCK!

- Broken glass and nails - OUCH!

In the city over the summer, on hot days, I can't cross the street because the tar sticks to my wheels. Then everything sticks to my wheels."

I wrote and wrote and wrote. A few minutes later, my journal looked like the board the other day. So many disgusting things can get stuck to the wheels of a wheelchair.

Who knew?

Passing and Picking

The last practice before the start of the season was all about passing and picking.

"In order to play as a team," Coach Acevedo said as we huddled at midcourt, "we need to know how to pass the ball, and we need to know how to catch the ball."

First, we worked on chest passes and bounce passes. We focused on the basics—gripping the ball, aiming for a spot, stepping toward the target, and moving toward the ball. Then we ran some drills and played Monkey in the Middle and Bull in the Ring (which is really the same thing as Monkey in the Middle, just with a few more rules).

"We need to know what to do on the court when we don't have the ball," Coach Acevedo said after a water break. "That's all about setting screens."

Coach Acevedo explained what a screen was—a blocking move that helped a teammate get open. Next he showed us how to set a screen—by standing up straight and perfectly still with our feet a little more than shoulder-width apart and our arms crossed in front. Then he showed us what the person receiving the screen did—waited for the screen, faked in the opposite direction, and then ran shoulder-to-shoulder off the screen.

"That's the key," Coach Acevedo said. "Brush your teammate's shoulder. Your defender shouldn't have any room to get around it. Explode off that screen!"

"Explode?" Red said.

"It's an expression," I said. "It means run real hard."

"Got it. Run real hard."

We ran through a few pick drills, but by this point, all anyone could think about was the last part of practice:

Uniforms.

24 and 32

Coach Acevedo gave out the jerseys while everyone was taking foul shots. I was shooting with Red, and he was on the line when, with my basketball eyes, I spotted Coach Acevedo heading our way.

"How's it going over here?" he asked.

"Red's on fire again," I said. "He's made eight in a row."

At the stripe, Red was midroutine. He took three low dribbles, spun the ball, looked at the rim, extended his arms, and took the underhanded shot.

Swish.

"Nine!" I gave him a pound.

"Nine in a row and twenty-two for twenty-five." Red grinned. "That's eighty-eight percent. Last time, I shot twenty for twenty-five. That's eighty percent. The time before that, I shot twenty-three for twenty-five. That's ninety-two percent."

"Blake Daniels is Clifton United's free-throw-shooting machine," Coach Acevedo said.

"Mason Irving's a good free-throw shooter, too," Red said. "So far, he's thirteen for twenty. That's sixty-five percent. He has five more shots to go. Last time, he shot fourteen for twenty-five. That's fifty-six percent. The time before that, he shot—"

"You two want your uniforms?" Coach Acevedo interrupted.

"Oh, yeah!" Red charged over. "Did I get number twenty-four?" He hopped from foot to foot. "Rick Barry wore number number twenty-four. Rick Barry shot free throws underhanded. He shot eighty-nine percent from the free-throw line. He made—"

"Here you go," Coach Acevedo said.

He reached into the duffel on his shoulder, pulled out a shirt, and handed it to Red.

Red stared at the navy tee. He traced the words *Clifton United* written in gold cursive on the front. Then he turned the shirt over and traced DANIELS written in gold block letters across the top. Then he traced the number twenty-four beneath it.

"Wow," Red whispered. "Thank you, Coach Acevedo."

"You're welcome, Red."

Red showed me the shirt.

"Boo-yah!" I hammer-fisted the air.

"What uniform number did Mason Irving get?"

Coach Acevedo reached into the bag and pulled out my shirt.

"Number thirty-two!" Red raised both arms. "You got Rip Hamilton's number!"

Coach Acevedo tossed me the shirt.

"Thanks, Coach," I said.

The Games Begin

Just three days later, we were putting on our uniforms for real.

"Let's get this season started," Coach Acevedo said.

I checked the gym. Edgemont's gym looked nothing like RJE's. Banners and pennants for volleyball titles and track and field records and soccer championships and basketball victories covered the walls. A scoreboard hung above the bleachers, and there were fans in those bleachers, too. Yeah, Edgemont had actual fans, at least thirty or forty, all sitting directly across from the home team's bench.

For us, only Emily's dad and Mehdi's parents had made the trip.

"Bring it in, United." Coach Acevedo waved his iPad. We huddled up in front of the first row of bleachers, our bench. "I see the way some of you are looking around the gym and sizing up the other team. Let's relax. On game days, I'm a big believer in body language. If you're hanging your head and slumping your shoulders, your opponent's going to see that and take advantage of it." He pointed to the court. "No matter what happens out there, no hanging heads and no slumping shoulders."

Everyone clapped.

"I couldn't care less about the score today. I only want to see Clifton United playing hard and having fun. We play defense, we rebound the basketball, we have fun." He kicked up the ball from under his foot. "I'm super pumped for our season. You should be, too."

"Oh, yeah!" Red said, doing his hop. "Let's go, Clifton United!"

"When that whistle blows and that ball goes up," Coach Acevedo said, "we show this league just how tight Clifton United is. Whether you're on the floor or on the bench, everyone contributes. Everyone."

＊ ＊ ＊

The game didn't start out so hot. Actually, it was a total disaster.

After the first quarter, we trailed 10–0.

"We're getting shut out," Red said. "Has there ever been a shutout in basketball?"

"I don't think so," I said, "but that could change."

"What if we get shut out?" He pinky-thumbed his leg.

"We still have three quarters left, Red. We won't."

"What if we do?" He hunched forward and swayed. "What if we get shut out, Mason Irving?"

I put my hand on his leg. "We won't."

We didn't.

A few minutes into the second quarter, Jason boxed out his man and grabbed the rebound. He passed to Keith, who dribbled by his defender and drove the length of the court for a layup.

"Time-out! Time-out!" Coach Acevedo raced onto the floor. He jumping-body-bumped the players in the game and high-fived everyone on the bench. "That's what I'm talking about! Rebounds lead to baskets."

Red was as fired up as Coach Acevedo. He gave everyone double-fisted pounds, and then we busted out our handshake:

"Right hand, left hand, elbow, elbow." We said the steps. "Fist, fist, knuckles, blow it up. Spin, jump, bump . . .

"Boo-yah!"

But Keith's basket was pretty much our only highlight for the next two quarters. We trailed 25–4 at the half and 34–6 after three.

Still, Coach Acevedo was true to his word. He said he couldn't care less about the score, and he meant it. Even though Edgemont was running us out of their gym, he never stopped cheering. To be perfectly honest, at times he sounded *delusional*. I'd looked up what *delusional* meant. It means totally unrealistic.

Red cheered us on, too. Whenever we scored a basket or made a stop, he stomped the bleachers, waved his towel, and cheered harder than anyone.

But that wasn't very often. Most of the time, he snapped his towel or covered his face with it.

I ran the point to start the fourth quarter. On our first possession, I passed to Wil on the wing. On the release, Maya popped out and screened my man. I brushed Maya's shoulder and *exploded* to the hoop. Wil hit me with the pass. I put up a floater.

Swish!

"Mason Irving scores!" Red shouted. "Your first points!" He waved his towel like a lasso. "Way to go, Mason Irving!"

I pumped my fist at Red and sprinted back on defense.

Believe it or not, for the rest of the game, we played decent. Yeah, Edgemont was playing their second- and third-stringers, but we were getting stops and coming through on offense. Maya scored her first basket, Keith sank a pair of free throws, and I hit a shot from the baseline.

* * *

"Here's how we're going to look at today's game," Coach Acevedo said in the huddle after the postgame handshake. "Yeah, we've got our work cut out for us. There's no two ways about that. But each and every one of you showed me something in that fourth quarter." He held up the iPad. "Now I know I said I couldn't care less about the score, but I want you to see this anyway. Check out the quarter-by-quarter breakdown of the scoring."

"10–0 in the first quarter," Red said. "15–4 in the second quarter, 9–2 in the third quarter, 8–8 in the fourth quarter." He rattled off the scores even before Coach Acevedo swiped the screen.

"That's right, Red," Coach Acevedo said. "We tied in the fourth quarter. That means we're capable of holding our own in this league. We will put together four good quarters. We will win this season. I guarantee it."

Bulldozed and Blitzed

Our next game was against O'Malley. We got bulldozed, 36–19. Then we got blitzed by Crystal Lake, 32–14. Just like that, we were 0–3.

Still, Coach Acevedo stayed positive as ever, and after the Crystal Lake game, he singled out Red.

"Every team needs a Blake Daniels," he said. "I love the energy you bring to our bench. I love your attitude. You never stop cheering. You embody what it means to be a teammate, and if any of you don't know what *embody* means, look it up when you get home."

I think *embody* meant to show.

But the thing is, Red did stop cheering. A lot. Most of the time, he had his clasped hands behind his neck and his arms pressed to his head. For the last quarter of the O'Malley game, he draped his towel over his head. And during the second half of the Crystal Lake game, he wore his old-man face.

I *hated* seeing the old-man face at basketball.

After singling out Red, Coach Acevedo repeated what he had said after the Edgemont game:

"We will win this season," he said. "I guarantee it."

Guarantee?

We'd dropped our first three games by a combined score of 110–47, and our next game was against Millwood, the best team in the league.

Nasty Notecards

That same week we were getting our butts handed to us on the basketball court, it was a whole new ballgame for Avery and me. Believe it or not, things were looking up.

We were working on our project. Yeah, that's right, working on our project. Together. We were calling it "The Nasty Nine," about the nine grossest things that have ever gotten stuck to Avery's chair.

We spent most of the week researching them, putting the information on notecards, and creating our outline, just like Mr. Acevedo showed us at the conference. At first, we didn't find much, but Mr. Acevedo insisted we keep digging around and "amp up the nasty."

We did.

The grossest thing we learned about had to do with movie theaters: Fecal matter is everywhere, and by fecal matter, I mean poop. Yeah, poop. But it's not on the floor. You're not stepping on it or rolling through it. You're sitting in it!

Here's how it happens: When some people use the bathroom, they don't wash their hands. Then when they go back to their seats, they touch the armrests, cup holders, and cushions . . . none of which are ever washed or cleaned.

Nasty!

Back-to-School Night

Back-to-School Night was on Thursday that week, but Mom couldn't make it because it was on the same night as Back-to-School Night at her school, which is how it is every year.

Mom's fine about missing Back-to-School Night because it's usually crowded, and there's never really an opportunity to talk with the teacher. The night is more for those parents who want to hear the teacher go over the class expectations, which my mom already knows.

"He's going to have a long night," Mom said that morning. "Some of those parents are going to give him quite the earful about test prep."

Mom's not fine about missing family conferences. That's what we call parent conferences at RJE. They're called family conferences because kids are encouraged to attend, and in Lesley Irving's world, *encouraged to attend* means *expected to attend*. They're not for another couple months, but

Mom's already made it known just how much she's looking forward to sitting down one-on-one with Mr. Acevedo.

"One-on-one?" I said, the last time she brought it up. "Me, you, and Mr. Acevedo—that's three of us. How can that be one-on-one? Does that mean I don't have to go?"

Her look was her answer. I still had to go.

Singled Out

"For CC today," Mr. Acevedo said on Friday morning, "I want to acknowledge some of the project work I've seen this week."

He sat cross-legged in his spot on the carpet. I sat on the couch between Red and Sebi.

"Are we dazzling you, Teach?" Declan asked.

"You most certainly are, and I want to single a few of you out, but before I do, I want to say a few words about last night's Back-to-School Night." He chuckled. "It was standing room only in here."

"Did you walk on the tables and read to the parents?" Diego asked, swinging the strings on his hat.

"Not exactly." Mr. Acevedo shook his head. "Your parents had lots of questions and ideas. Lots of them. They like to have a say about what goes on in the classroom." He chuckled again. "I'm going to see what I can do about meeting some of their expectations. Now let me single a few of you out. I'm starting with Gavin."

"What did I do?" Gavin asked.

"I'll tell you what," Mr. Acevedo said. "You're making some outstanding real-world connections. I'm super pumped you and Mariam are researching MREs."

"What are MREs?" Lana and Jordan asked at the same time.

Mr. Acevedo motioned to Gavin.

"Meals Ready-to-Eat," he said. "MREs. That's what people in the military eat. They can be pretty disgusting."

Gavin's father served in Afghanistan. Each year, he leads the Veterans' Day ceremony at RJE. Gavin's notebooks are covered with photographs of his father and other soldiers. Sometimes Gavin wears a dog-tag necklace.

Mr. Acevedo turned to Hunter. "Would you say a few words about your topic?"

"I'm working with Attie," he said. "Our topic is musical instruments."

"They're covered in germs," Attie said. "It's so gross."

"We're still deciding which instruments we're going to write about," Hunter said. "Definitely the piano and guitar."

Hunter plays the piano and guitar. He's amazing at both.

"I had no idea instruments were so filthy." Mr. Acevedo recrossed his legs and grabbed his ankles. "Their topic is fascinating." He turned to Avery. "So is yours. Will you share a little?"

"Do I have to?"

"I'd like you to. With whom are you working?"

She pointed to me.

"What's your topic?"

"Our topic . . . our topic is my wheelchair."

My wheelchair.

Everyone knew that was our topic, but I don't think anyone had ever heard Avery say those two words before.

"What about your wheelchair?"

Avery curled her lip. "The nasty stuff that gets stuck to my wheels."

"Noah," Mr. Acevedo said, "let's hear about your topic."

"I'm working with Lana." Noah wiped his chin with his sleeve. "Our topic is my brother's booger wall."

"Your what?" Trinity asked.

"My brother's booger wall."

"Sick!" Danny said. "My cousin has one of those."

"What's a booger wall?" Grace asked.

"My little brother picks his nose." Noah wiped his chin again. "Then he puts the boogers on the wall behind my parents' bedroom door. My mother found the wall over the summer and flipped out."

"Dude, that's friggin' foul," Avery said.

Noah nodded. "He still walks around with his finger up his nose, but we have no idea where he's putting the boogers."

"He's eating them!" Zachary said.

Everyone laughed.

"On that *appetizing* note," Mr. Acevedo said, "that's a wrap for CC." He strummed the carpet. "Next week, I need to make a few changes to the project."

"What kind of changes?" Piper asked.

"You'll find out Monday."

In the Amp

To end the week, Mr. Acevedo held T3 outside in the amphitheater.

He read us a short story about this kid who had the same first and last name, Murphy Murphy. The kid had the worst luck in the world. He also had really bad stage fright, but he agreed to be in a skit for the drama club because he really liked a girl.

I sat in the first row on the end between Red and Mr. Goldberg. When we arrived, Mr. Goldberg was emptying the garbage cans next to the playground. He decided to join us.

As Mr. Acevedo read, he walked up and down the steps and back and forth along the rows. He hopped onto the benches and tiptoed around us, twisting and turning and dipping like a dancer.

When there were only a couple pages left—when he got to the scene where Murphy Murphy was bumbling through

the skit—he walked over to the jungle gym and read from the deck at the top of the climbing wall. Then when he finished, he closed the book and bowed like a conductor in front of an orchestra.

Everyone applauded.

Some of the kids stood and cheered.

I did.

Double-Teamed

"This turkey burger is delicious, Rip's Mom," Red said.

I bumped his shoulder. "You say everything she makes is delicious."

"Everything is."

"I agree." Mom burger-pounded him across the island.

"Quit playing with your food, you two," I said.

We were on the stools in the kitchen having dinner: turkey burgers on challah bread with sweet potato fries. Just like always when Red stayed for dinner on Saturdays.

Red was also sleeping over because Suzanne had to work the night shift at the hospital. Up until a few months ago, Red never slept over. He only slept in his own bed. But back in June, he said he wanted to stay over one night, and it went fine . . . though it definitely didn't hurt that we played Xbox until the sun came through the basement window.

"I'm looking forward to finally meeting Mr. Acevedo," Mom said.

"That's not until next Saturday," I said. "You're looking forward to it already?" I half smiled. "I think someone needs to add a little excitement to her life."

"We have a game next Saturday," Red said. "A home game against O'Malley at nine o'clock. We have to be there at eight-thirty."

"That's when I'm meeting him," Mom said. "Same with Suzanne."

"You'll get to see his tattoos," Red said, swiveling. "The butterfly one on his leg is so cool. It's all different colors—red, green, yellow, blue, black. He has this other tattoo that says—"

"We play Millwood on Wednesday," I interrupted.

"An away game at Millwood on Wednesday," Red added. "Millwood's the best team in the league."

I popped a couple fries into my mouth. "It could get ugly."

"Still with the attitude?" Mom said.

"I'm just being realistic. Coach Acevedo keeps guaranteeing we're going to win, but I don't know. We only have five games left and two of them are against Millwood."

"An away game at Millwood on Wednesday, October second," Red said, swiveling faster. "A home game against Voigt on Saturday, October fifth, an away game against Rolling Hills on Monday, October fourteenth, an away game at Lockport on Tuesday, October fifteenth, a home game against Millwood on Saturday, October nineteenth."

Mom tapped my plate. "You up-to-date with the project?"

I nodded.

"Is that a yes?"

"Yes, Mom."

"You checked the webpage?" She looked at both of us.

We didn't reply.

"You need to," she said. "Your outline is due, and you have another conference coming up. Mr. Acevedo posted a checklist for it."

"This is where you say you wished all your teachers were this organized."

"Don't be so fresh." She pointed a fry.

I leaned across the island and tried to bite it, but she pulled it back.

"You're writing your page next week, right after the conference," Mom said. "This project is moving quickly. You don't want to fall behind."

"You've told me a gazillion times," I said.

"Xander McDonald and I finished our outline," Red said. "Xander and I had fourteen notecards. Ms. Yvonne helped us."

"Ms. Yvonne's coming into the class again?" Mom said. "She started doing push-in?"

Red shook his head. "I see her out of class."

"We had ELA on the playground the other day," I said. "She worked with Red and X then."

"Mr. Acevedo's making changes to the project," Red said. "He's telling us what they are on Monday."

"I'm sure that has something to do with Back-to-School Night. I heard some of the parents were relentless." She motioned to my plate. "You done?"

I piled mine on top of hers.

Red popped a last fry into his mouth and then added his to the stack.

"As soon as we're done cleaning up from dinner," Mom said, heading for the compost, "we're going over your folder."

"Why?" I half whined.

"Because I said so. I don't need to give you a reason."

I let out a puff. Sometimes my teacher-mom needed to be a little less hands-on.

"I want to look at your project folder, too, Red," she said.

"Thanks, Rip's Mom."

I bumped his shoulder again. "You really aren't normal."

He bumped me back and then started swiveling again.

"After we check your folder," Mom said as she scraped a plate, "we're going to do something about all those clothes on your floor."

"What are we going to do about them?"

"Stop showing off in front of Red." She shot me a look. "You're being fresh again."

I brushed my locks off my forehead and let out another puff.

"I know *your* room doesn't have clothes all over it," she said to Red. "Maybe you can help Rip clean his room."

"No, thanks, Rip's Mom."

Shaking Things Up

Back on Friday, we ended the week in the Amp. Today, we started the week in the Amp.

"We interrupt Room 208 for a special bulletin!" Mr. Acevedo said. He stood with a leg on the front bench and his iPad on his knee. "I need to make a couple changes to the project. I have to shake things up a little bit."

"I don't understand," Piper said.

"That's because I haven't explained it yet, Piper. This week, you and your partner will be writing a persuasive essay. It's an additional writing assignment, a short one. You'll need to follow a particular format." He paused. "Hopefully, this will please some of your parents." He nodded to Avery, whose hand was up.

"Can I say something?" she said.

"Is it about this writing assignment?"

"Yes and no."

Mr. Acevedo looked at her sideways. "Then I'll say maybe."

"I'm not the only one who thinks this," she said. "Can I use the T-word?"

"If you must." Mr. Acevedo placed the iPad on the bench.

I checked Red. He sat at the end of the second row next to Mr. Goldberg, who'd joined us again, even though we weren't having T3. Red was already hunched forward and pinky-thumbing his legs.

"What's on your mind, Ms. Goodman?" Mr. Acevedo said, stepping to the front of the Amp.

"We do test prep every day in math."

"You do."

"The third and fourth graders do test prep every day in ELA."

"They do."

She rolled her eyes. "The fifth graders at all the other schools do test prep. How are we going to do well on the tests if we don't know how to take them?"

"We're learning." Mr. Acevedo toed the sand with his sneaker.

"We're not learning the questions on the test."

"We're learning," he said. "We're learning more than just the answers to some questions on a test. We're learning . . ." He stopped midsentence and pulled back his hair. "Show of hands—how many of you feel the same way as Ms. Goodman? Be honest."

A few hands went up.

Then a few more.

And a few more.

Then mine.

"We're learning," Mr. Acevedo said. He drew a circle in the air with his finger. "But we're learning in a way that doesn't stifle creativity, and if you don't know what *stifle* means, look it up."

I didn't know what *stifle* meant, but from the sound of it, I didn't want it happening to me.

Down the row, Red swayed from side to side.

"I understand I need to make adjustments," Mr. Acevedo said, kicking at the sand. "Your parents have made that perfectly clear. But I'm not turning Room 208 into a test-prep mill, no matter how much noise anyone makes. I guarantee that."

It was the first time I'd ever heard Mr. Acevedo speak with an edge.

I checked Red again—hunched over, swaying, and wearing his old-man face.

"We learn best when we're having fun," Mr. Acevedo said, keeping the tone. "We learn best when we're doing. That's how we learn how to think. Learning how to answer specific questions for a test—that's not learning. That's . . . I don't know what that is."

Mr. Acevedo pulled back his hair again and looked around. He made eye contact with a few of us.

"When you teach to a test," he said, softening his words, "you program the test taker to respond to a question in a narrow way. When you teach a real skill—when you learn a real skill—the person learning the skill is able to apply that skill in all different contexts." He stepped to Avery. "Did that answer your question, Ms. Goodman?"

"Whatever," she said.

"For what it's worth," he said, tapping her armrest, "that was a healthy interruption. I'm glad you brought that up. Now let's get back to where we were—the new persuasive essay. That's the first change to the project. The second change takes place in two weeks. Each group will now be presenting to the class. We're going to have oral presen—"

"No!" Red shouted. He stood up and shook his head violently. "No, I can't. I can't. It's too much. It's too much." He covered his head with his arms. "No!"

He took off.

I Survived

I tore out of the playground and headed for the gym door where Red ran into the school. I darted across the gym and through the cafeteria, but there was no sign of him.

I charged down the main hall.

"Slow down, Mr. Irving," Ms. Waldon called from her desk by the announcement monitor.

"Did Red come by?" I asked, speed-walking up.

"Is everything all right?" She pointed down the K-1 hallway. "He just went upstairs."

I bolted past without answering and headed for the staircase. I pulled open the door, two-at-a-timed the steps, and then bounded into the second floor hall.

No Red.

I headed straight for Room 208.

That's where I found him. He stood by the back table in front of Bryan's seat. He had taken down the silver toolbox with the *I Survived* books from atop the cubbies.

"*I Survived the Attacks of September 11, 2001,*" he said, removing the book from the toolbox and putting it on the desk. He then lifted out a second book. "*I Survived the Nazi Invasion, 1944.*" He placed it on top of the first.

"Red." I walked up. "Red."

"*I Survived Hurricane Katrina, 2005.*" He kept stacking books. "*I Survived the Battle of Gettysburg, 1863.*"

"Red," I said again. I moved next to him.

"*I Survived the Japanese Tsunami, 2011.*"

"Red, what's up?"

"I can't," he said without looking up. "I can't. It's too

much, too much. *I Survived the San Francisco Earthquake, 1906.*"

"What is?" I placed my hand on his back. "What's too much?"

"It's too much." He shook his head faster. "It's too much. I can't . . . I can't get up in front of the class. It's too much, too much."

I let out a puff. "I'm sure . . . Red, Mr. Acevedo's cool. He won't make you get . . ."

Mr. Acevedo and Ms. Yvonne rushed in.

"*I Survived the Sinking of the* Titanic, *1912*," Red continued. "*I Survived the Bombing of Pearl Harbor, 1941.*"

"Honey, what's wrong?" Ms. Yvonne asked. She stepped up to Red like only she could.

"It's too much," he said, squinching his face. He started restacking the books. "*I Survived the Bombing of Pearl Harbor, 1941. I Survived the San Francisco Earthquake, 1906.*"

"Honey, look at me," Ms. Yvonne said softly. She placed a hand on the table next to the books. "Everything's okay. Look at me."

"*I Survived the Japanese Tsunami, 2011.*" He slowly looked up.

"Honey, everything's okay. I want you to come with me."

I checked Mr. Acevedo. He stood off to the side with his hands gripping his hair.

"Come with me to my office, okay?" Ms. Yvonne placed her hand on the stack of books. "Come with me."

"Am I kicked off Clifton United?" Red asked, still shaking his head and squinting. "Am I kicked off Clifton United? Am I kicked off Clifton United?"

"Honey, no, of course not," she answered.

"Am I kicked off Clifton United?"

"No one's kicking you off anything, Red." Mr. Acevedo still held his hair. "Every team needs a Blake Daniels, remember?"

"You hear that, Red?" I touched his back again. "We need you on Clifton United. You're our free-throw-shooting machine."

"I can't get up in front of the class," Red said. "I can't get up in front of the class. Please don't kick me off the team."

"No one's making you get up in front of the class, Red." Ms. Yvonne glanced at Mr. Acevedo again.

"No one's making you do anything you don't want to," he said. "I guarantee it."

The H-Word

"Do you want to look at the instructions?" I said, tilting the iPad to Avery.

"Not really," she said. "I hate getting up in front of the class."

I flinched.

"Ooh." She wiggled her fingers. "I said the H-word at RJE. Calm down, dude. It's not like I shouted it across the cafeteria."

We were back in Room 208. I was in Melissa's seat across from Avery. After Red's episode, Mr. Acevedo decided to have the rest of class inside. Back in the room, he explained that he'd be holding conferences while we worked on our persuasive pieces and prepared for the presentations.

"They're not for another two weeks," I said. "And we only have to be in front of the class for a few minutes."

"I don't care if it's for a few seconds. It's getting up in front of the class. I *hate* getting up in front of the friggin' class."

"I'm beginning to sense that." I slid over a blank note-card and started darkening a corner. "I'll do the writing assignment, Avery," I said without looking up.

"Huh?"

"The persuasive essay. I'll do it." I still didn't look up. "It's an olive branch."

"A what?"

Even though I couldn't see her face, I knew she was curling her lip.

"It's an olive branch," I said again.

"Whatever, dude."

Massacre at Millwood

I knew we were in for it against Millwood, but I didn't realize just how much we were in for it until I pulled open the gym door.

No lie, Millwood's gym looked like one of those high school gyms you see in the movies. Fifteen rows of bleachers on both sides, baseline to baseline, and those bleachers were packed. Seriously packed. As the Millwood players warmed up, the fans waved orange and black towels and bobbed to the dubstep pumping out of the speakers on the walls behind the baskets. Championship banners hung from all the rafters. The only thing missing was a Jumbotron!

As we entered the gym . . .

"Boo!"

"Go back to Clifton!"

"Boo!"

"I've never been booed and heckled before," Keith said, cringing.

"Me neither," I said.

I ducked back into the hall and went over to Red. He was with Mehdi and Mikey and hadn't reached the door.

"It's loud in there, Red," I said.

"That's why I'm wearing my earplugs, Mason Irving." He tapped his ears.

"Really loud." I tried to say it like I meant it without freaking him out.

Red turtled his neck and pressed his earplugs.

"You ready?" I asked.

"Ready as I'll ever be, Mason Irving."

We stepped in.

You know how before a big UFC match the two fighters stare each other down and you think they're going to start whaling on each other right then and there? Well, every Millwood player looked like one of those fighters as we walked by their bench. They were ginormous, too. They looked like middle schoolers. Two of them even had mustaches.

The scariest member of Millwood was their coach. He was yelling, red-face yelling at his team.

"Take it to them!" Coach Crazy shouted. "What happened against Edgemont on Sunday was an embarrassment. You will not embarrass the orange and black on this court again!"

Over the weekend, Millwood lost to Edgemont. It was their first home loss in three seasons.

"Show this team what the orange and black is all about." Coach Crazy gripped the jersey of one of his players. "Take it to them! Stomp them out! Send this league a message."

I'd heard about coaches like Coach Crazy, but I'd never seen one in person. He freaked me out.

I checked Red: Fists by his squinting eyes. Swaying.

"How we doing over here, Red?" Coach Acevedo stepped to us.

"Their coach is buggin'," I said first.

Coach Acevedo nodded. "He sure is."

"Their coach is buggin', Mason Irving," Red said. "Seriously buggin'."

"Seriously buggin'."

* * *

"Let's relax, everyone," Coach Acevedo said in the pregame huddle. "Remember what I said about body language. No slumping shoulders or hanging heads. Whatever happens out there happens out there."

Coach Acevedo waved us closer.

"We're Clifton United," he said. "We're Clifton United before we take the court, we're Clifton United while we're on the court, we're Clifton United after we leave the court." He pointed down the gym. "That's not who we are. That's not who we want to be either." He rapped his chest. "We're Clifton United."

* * *

On the opening tip, Millwood's center easily out-jumped Jason and batted the ball to his mega-size teammate. Mega-Man lowered his shoulder and dribbled straight for Mikey and me. We were set in our chairs, but we couldn't stop Mega-Man. He drove *through* us and scored a layup.

"Press! Press!" Coach Crazy shouted. He waved his arms madly. "Press! Press!"

Press? A full-court press? Was he kidding?

I knew how to break a full-court press—we needed to spread the floor, make quick passes, and keep the ball in the middle. The thing is, most of my teammates had probably never even *heard* of a full-court press.

Jason tried inbounding to me, but Mega-Man bodied me out of the way, stole the pass, and fed a super-size team-mate. Super-Size lowered his shoulder, drove *through* Jason, and sank the layup.

That's pretty much how it went the entire first half.

Red didn't exactly enjoy it. He hid his eyes for most of

the first half. Either with his hands or a towel over his head. A couple times, when Coach Crazy was yelling stupid loud, he had his palms pressed to his ears as he shook his head.

I wanted to be in basketball mode, but Coach Crazy was in my head.

Because of what he was doing to Red.

Then Coach Crazy had his players start cherry-picking.

Midway through the second quarter, Millwood began playing defense with only four players. Whenever we had the ball on their end, they sent one player—a "cherry-picker"—to wait by our basket. As soon as they forced a turnover or grabbed a rebound, they threw the ball to Cherry-Picker for an easy hoop.

"Don't you think this is a little much?" Coach Acevedo said, walking down the sideline toward Coach Crazy.

Up until the cherry-picking, Coach Acevedo had been his positive, cheering self. But even Coach Acevedo had limits.

"Excuse me?" Coach Crazy said. He stood in front of the scorer's table with his arms folded across his Homer Simpson belly.

"Don't you think this type of gamesmanship is a little much?"

"Go back to your bench, Coach. Worry about your own team."

Coach Acevedo nodded once. "Thank you."

* * *

At halftime, Coach Acevedo brought us to an empty class-room away from the gym.

"Let's pick up those heads," he said. He closed the door and walked to the front of the room. "I don't want to see any hanging heads."

We all sat at the arm desks arranged in rows. He waited for everyone to look up.

"That's more like it." He smiled. He placed his iPad on the teacher's desk and pointed toward the hall. "What's happening out there has nothing to do with you. Nothing. It has everything to do with that coach. That coach is a bully, and if it were up to me, he wouldn't be coaching kids. Unfortunately, it's not up to me, so for another half, we have to deal with him."

With my basketball eyes, I checked Red, sitting diagonally across the aisle in the row along the windows. He was pinky-thumbing his thigh faster than I'd ever seen him. Both knees bounced against the desk. His wide eyes were glued to Coach Acevedo.

"Why doesn't the ref do something?" Keith asked.

"There's not much he can do," Coach Acevedo said. "That coach is not breaking the rules. He's just being a jerk." He pulled back his hair. "So here's what we're going to do."

Coach Acevedo picked up his iPad. "At our last practice, we worked on making passes and setting screens." He flipped open the cover, tapped the screen, and drew with his finger. "Making passes and setting screens. That's our strategy."

He held up the display.

"We're playing keep-away out there," he said. "Passing and picking away. Nonstop. It's not going to get us a lot of points, but it will run time off the clock, and it will keep them from scoring as much."

Then Coach Acevedo diagrammed a break-the-press play and an inbounds-pass play. I wasn't all that sure either would work, but it was better than what we had now. Which was nothing.

"Whatever happens out there happens," Coach Acevedo said again. "But no matter what happens out there, we keep our body language. When you're on the floor, you're playing hard. When you're on the bench, you're cheering hard. We're Clifton United. Let's get back out there."

The team headed out of the room. When I reached the door, I turned around.

Red hadn't moved.

Meltdown

"Let's go, Red," I said, waving. I took a step back into the room.

"No," he said, shaking his head. "No."

I swallowed. "Okay."

"No." He stood up and shook his head faster. His voice grew louder. "No, no."

He walked toward the front of the class, and when he reached the wall, he turned around and headed back. He held his fists next to his face like a boxer blocking punches.

"Red," I said, standing by the teacher's desk. "Red."

He walked past. He wasn't hearing me.

I checked the door. I couldn't leave to go get help. I couldn't leave Red alone.

I grabbed the locks above my neck and let out a puff. Then I let out another.

Everyone would reach the gym in a minute or two. Someone would notice we weren't there. Someone would come looking for us.

"Red," I said again. "Red."

He paced.

Back and forth.

Finally, Mehdi appeared.

"Hey, Rip," he said, walking in. "What's going . . . what's the matter with Red?"

"Can you go get Coach Acevedo?"

"What's the matter?"

"Can you just get him?"

Mehdi took off.

Red paced.

Back and forth.

Finally, Coach Acevedo arrived.

"Hey, Rip," he said, swinging into the room. "What's going on?"

"I can't," Red said as soon as he heard Coach Acevedo's voice. He paced faster. "I can't, I can't." His fists rapped the sides of his head. "I can't, I can't."

"He's been like this the whole time," I said. "You need to call his mom."

"Red," Coach Acevedo said. "Are you—"

"You need to call his mom," I said again.

"I can't," Red said a little louder. "I can't, I can't."

Coach Acevedo pulled back his hair and stared at Red.

"Call her," I said.

He took out his cell.

"You're going to stay here with me until I get in touch with her," he said. "Once I do, you need to go back inside and tell Mr. Karmoune he needs to coach. He's watching the team."

"Mehdi's dad's going to coach us?"

"Well, I can't exactly leave Red, can I?" he snapped. He pulled back his hair again. "Rip, the team needs you on the court. If our new strategy has any chance of working, you need to be out there."

I nodded.

"Show Mr. Karmoune the iPad," Coach Acevedo said. "Explain to him what we drew up. Tell him I probably won't be out there for the second half."

I nodded again.

"Before you head out," Coach Acevedo said, "I want you to tell Red what you're doing. Tell him that I'll be staying with him until his mom gets here. I know he probably won't hear it, but I want you to say it anyway."

He dialed Suzanne.

Coach Crazier

The strategy worked!

We ran time off the clock and kept Millwood from scoring. That turned Coach Crazy into Coach Crazier. Less than two minutes into the second half, he called time-out.

"What are you doing out there?" he top-of-his-lungs screamed. "You call that Millwood basketball?"

Less than two minutes later, he called another time-out.

"Do you want to play for Millwood?" he shouted at Super-Size and Mega-Man. "Do you?" He shook his hands over his head. "It doesn't look like it, and if you keep playing like that, you won't for much longer!"

I was in full basketball mode, playing my heart out and being there for my team, just like Coach Acevedo said I needed to be. The more Coach Crazier yelled, the more I got into it. Same with everyone on our bench.

"Keep a-way!" we chanted. "Keep a-way!"

The ref appreciated what we were doing.

"Way to move the ball around," he said several times.
"Way to play as a team."

After the final horn, he came over to our bench.

"Way to make the best of an ugly situation," he said.
"Your coach would've been proud of you. I'll be sure to let
him know how well you played. You handled yourselves
with class and dignity."

Millwood didn't.

They left us hanging at center court. Coach Crazier led
his team out of the gym without lining up for the postgame
handshake.

Fallout

The next morning after CC, Avery and I were first to conference with Mr. Acevedo. We talked in the meeting area by the bathtub.

"How are you holding up?" Mr. Acevedo asked me.

"I guess okay," I said, twisting a lock above my ear.

"Tough evening." Mr. Acevedo rubbed his eye with his palm. "I'm just glad Red's doing better."

I checked the back table. Ms. Yvonne was sitting with Red, Xander, and a few other kids. It was the first time all year she'd been in Room 208.

"Dude, I heard you lost by fifty." Avery swatted my shoulder.

"Was it that close?" I said.

"It wasn't exactly a great moment in sportsmanship." Mr. Acevedo recrossed his legs and grabbed his ankles. "If I'd been there for the second half, I don't know if I'd have been able to control myself with that coach."

"I can't believe we play them again in a couple weeks," I said.

"I should go," Avery said. "Is it at RJE?"

I nodded.

"I've never been to a basketball game." She swatted me again. "It'll be fun watching you get eaten alive."

"I feel sorry for the kids on that team," Mr. Acevedo said. "I'm really surprised the parents put up with that." He strummed the carpet. "Let's get down to business. Tell me what you got."

"We came up with a cool idea for our persuasive essay," I said, even though I'd done all the work. "We made up these two scientist characters, Dr. Icky-Icky and Dr. Poo-Poo." I peeked at Avery. "They're having a conversation about wheelchair wheels, how they're like magnets."

"They are like magnets," Avery said, nodding along. "They attract everything."

"I like that," Mr. Acevedo said.

"Their conversation convinces the reader to check out our page. When we do our oral presentation, we're going to dress up like them."

"Sounds good to me."

I opened my folder. "This is what our page is going to look like. We're making a wheelchair web. The middle of the page is going to have a picture of a wheelchair."

"We're putting the main idea on the backrest," Avery said, peeking at me. "All of the Nasty Nine information will go around it."

"Nice! I like that, too! You two look like you're all set." He palmed the floor and pushed himself up. "Let me go take a lap. See how everyone is doing. Then when I get back, we'll go over your outlines and folders."

"Mr. Acevedo," I said, before he stepped away, "can I get a book recommendation for Choice?"

"Coming right up, Rip."

He pointed at me with both index fingers and then headed for the realistic-fiction bins on the windowsill. Then he walked over to the milk crates on top of the cubbies. He returned with a stack.

"I only needed one," I said.

He tossed me *From the Notebooks of Melanin Sun.*

"It's short," I said, fanning the pages.

"Lots to think about." He held up the other books. "I'm going to leave these on your desk. This is your preview pile. When you finish that one, look through these. We'll have a conversation about your next book."

"Is he the reason you think I should read this?" I asked.

The cover had a picture of a boy holding a book through a window. He was black with hair like mine.

Mr. Acevedo laughed. "I forgot that Melanin had locks."

"Melanin? That's the kid's name?"

"Melanin Sun." Mr. Acevedo nodded. "Give it a shot. Let me know what you think. The book's a little more teen than you're used to reading, but you're ready for it. It's something you should read." He tapped my shoulder. "Thanks for helping yesterday. I don't know what I would've done without you."

I shrugged. "I'm just glad he's still on the team."

After the game, we had all met—Suzanne, Red, Coach Acevedo, me, and my mom. Yeah, my mom was there, too. She came with Suzanne.

Red was still on the team. Everyone made that clear right away. But moving forward, we were going to take things one game at a time. The next game was a home game, and Suzanne would be there for it. After that, we would wait and see.

"Red's lucky to have you," Mr. Acevedo said. "You're a good friend."

"He would've done the same for me."

A Must-Win

We needed a win today. If we were going to win this season, it had to be against Voigt, the only other team in the league that hadn't won. After today, we only had three games left—back-to-back away games against Rolling Hills and Lockport and the rematch against Millwood.

Yeah, we needed a win today.

"The second half of our season starts now," Coach Acevedo said in the pregame huddle. "We're putting that last game behind us. Rip, Maya, Keith, Alex, and Jason—you're our starting five." He motioned to the stage. "I know everyone's parents are here this morning, so everyone will get plenty of action today. When we're out there, we're playing defense and rebounding the basketball. Don't worry about the score."

Don't worry?

I was worried about the score. I wanted everyone else to worry about the score, too.

Today was our shot at a W.

On the first possession of the game, I dribbled down the left side and passed to Keith. He took a shot from the foul line extended.

Brick.

But Jason was standing under the hoop and caught the ball as if it was a pass. He put it right up and sank the layup.

"Our first lead of the season!" Red jumped onto his seat. "Our first lead! Our first lead!"

But our first lead didn't last very long. Voigt scored the next three baskets and went ahead, 6–2.

Still, we kept the game close. Midway through the quarter, I snuck up behind their big man, stripped him of the ball, and fed Maya for a breakaway. Then in the last minute, Alex drained a jumper from the elbow.

After one, Voigt led 9–8.

At the half, they led 18–15.

"That was the best we've played all season," Coach Acevedo said at halftime. "Rip, way to keep the ball moving. Maya and Keith, great hustle as usual. Alex, Mehdi, Mikey, Emily—way to be ready off the bench. Let's keep this going!"

To start the second half, the starting five were back on the court, and we continued to play like a team. Keith and I ran a textbook give-and-go play, Maya and Jason ran a picture-perfect pick-and-roll play, and on one possession, all five of us touched the ball before we scored.

Heading into the final minutes of the third, it was a one-point game.

That's when things fell apart.

Voigt went on a 10–0 run and opened up an eleven-point lead. We matched them basket-for-basket the rest of the way, but we could never manage to get within ten until Leslie scored her first points of the season with forty-four seconds left.

By then, it was too late.

We lost our fifth straight, 32–24.

* * *

Following the postgame handshake, Coach Acevedo led us onto the stage.

"Thank you for coming this morning," he said to the parents. "It was super exciting having you here. You even got to see us hold our first lead of the season."

"For like a minute," I muttered.

"A minute's better than nothing, Rip." Coach Acevedo clapped. "We're making progress. I'm super proud of each and every player on Clifton United."

"Me, too," Red said.

All the parents laughed. Some applauded.

"Can anyone tell me what I said in the huddle after our first game?" Coach Acevedo asked. He nodded to Red.

" 'We're capable of holding our own in this league.' " Red hopped. " 'We will put together four good quarters, and we will win this season. I guarantee it.' " He shook his fists next to his eyes. "I mean, I didn't say I guarantee it. You said I guarantee it, Coach Acevedo." He covered his face.

"That's exactly what I said, Red." Coach Acevedo drew a circle in the air. "I guaranteed we'd win this season, and I'm not wavering. I'm saying it again right here in front of all the parents. We will win this season. I guarantee it."

Guarantee?

Happy Writing Day!

At CC on Monday morning, Mr. Acevedo said we were taking a day off from the projects. He told us to get our writer's notebooks and head out to the Amp.

"We're kicking off the week with one of *mi abuela*'s sayings," he said. " *'El medio más fácil para ser engañado es creerse más listo que los demás.'* Any of my translators want to give that one a shot?" He pointed with his elbow to Zachary.

"The easiest way to be fooled is to believe you're smarter than the rest," Zachary said.

"Exactly." Mr. Acevedo hopped over the first-row bench and gave Zachary a pound. "What does that mean?" He motioned to Ana.

"You shouldn't think you're smarter than everyone else," she said.

"Because?" He motioned for her to continue.

"Because you'll be fooled if you do."

"Exactly, Ana." He strummed his chest. "We all bring

something unique to Room 208. No one's better, no one's smarter, but we're all different." He adjusted an earring. "Today, we're going to write about what makes us different, what makes us unique. Today is Writing Day! We're writing like we did that first week when we stood on our tables."

"Or ladder," Avery said.

"Or ladder, Ms. Goodman."

I checked Red. He sat next to Ms. Yvonne in the row behind me. Ms. Yvonne smiled when she saw me looking their way. Red waved.

"We can write about anything?" Piper asked.

"So long as it's connected to what makes you different or unique."

"Can we draw?" Sebi asked.

"So long as the drawing has captions or thought bubbles," Mr. Acevedo said. "There needs to be some text." He motioned to the playground. "Go find yourself a place to write. Let's get poppin'."

Unique

I'm the black kid with the hair who lives and breathes basketball.

That's who I am. So they tell me.

She's the kid in the wheelchair. He's the kid who's crazy about the Beatles. She's the kid who loves Hello Kitty. He's the milatary kid. She's the theater kid. He's the kid who wears hats with earflaps. She's the kid who runs track. He's the kid who calls everyone by there first name and there last name. He's the man with the piercings and tattoos and who looks like he in a rock band.

That's how people see us, that's how we see one an other, that's who we are.

That's not who we are.

I'm so much more.

A Very Good Man

Avery and I kicked butt on our project this week. We wrote the persuasive essay and finished the final draft of our page. All we had left to do was work on the oral presentation. We were doing that this weekend.

Mr. Acevedo needed to conference with all the groups today to go over another schedule change. The oral presentations were supposed to start on Monday—it still said so on the due-date chart—but they were now starting on Wednesday because Mr. Acevedo had to attend a teacher-training workshop.

"For the life of me," he said when he told us, "I don't understand why they schedule these things during the school day. It's disruptive and disrespectful. I'd much rather be in here with you than have to sit through two days of PowerPoints and lectures."

We weren't going to have a sub while Mr. Acevedo was out. We were going to have two days of extra math and science.

I lay on the carpet with my legs across a beanbag chair. Avery sat parked beside the bathtub. We were up next, waiting to conference with Mr. Acevedo.

Suddenly, I shot up.

"No way!" I spun to Avery.

"What?" she said.

I scrambled across the carpet and sat on the lip of the tub. "Your name," I said.

"What about it?"

"I figured it out."

She squeezed her brakes. "Dude, what are you talking about?"

"Avery Goodman." I tapped her name on the front of her project folder.

"So?"

She knew what I was talking about. I could tell. She knew *exactly* what I was talking about.

"Avery Goodman," I said again. "A very—"

"Don't!" She cut me off. "Come with me." She wheeled for the door. "Mr. Acevedo," she said, interrupting Noah and Lana's conference, "we'll be in the hall."

I followed her out.

"Who told you?" she asked, hockey-stopping in front of the stairs.

"No one."

"Someone had to tell you."

"Honest, no one did." I smiled. "A very good man. Avery Goodman."

"You can't tell anyone."

"Why not?"

"Dude!" She rolled into my leg.

"Ouch." I jumped back.

"You can't tell anyone."

"Okay." I laughed. "But I don't see what's the big deal about—"

"I'm serious, dude. I don't want people to know."

"Okay, I heard you." I still smiled.

"I don't want people to know," she said again. She lowered her voice. "You're my first friend to figure it out."

"What did you just say?"

"I said you're the first one to figure it out."

"No, that's not what you said." I smiled more. "You said I was your first *friend* to figure it out."

"No, I didn't." She squeezed her brakes.

"Yes, you did, Avery. You called me your friend."

"No, I . . . well, I meant anyone."

"You meant friend."

"Whatever, dude."

Speedy and Ri-Dic-U-Lous

"It should be a good one here this afternoon, folks," I announced while rebounding during the pregame shoot-around. "We're coming to you live this Monday afternoon from Rolling Hills Elementary, where the Red Raiders of Rolling Hills will be taking on Clifton United."

Up until we walked into their gym, I didn't think we had a chance. I thought our last chance of winning was against Voigt. But as soon as I saw the Rolling Hills players, that changed. Size-wise, they were no bigger than us, and they had three girls on their squad, too.

"Maya dribbles to the corner," I play-by-played. "She shoots . . . it's good!" I batted the rebound back her way. "Maya's got the rock again. She passes to Red. Red sends it to Emily. She drives across the lane . . . yes!"

Red had his earplugs in. He also had his headphones under his chair on the sidelines. He was allowed to be here even though Suzanne wasn't. He'd been fine ever since the Millwood game, and all the grown-ups—Suzanne, Ms. Yvonne, Mr. Acevedo—thought he should be at the game.

Right now, he was wearing his basketball smile.

"Mehdi sizes up his shot," I announced. "He shoots . . . he banks it home! Glass action!" I fed Keith at the top of the key. "Keith fakes left, he clears some space, he shoots . . . nothing but net!"

If we played like this during the game, we had a chance.

We never had a chance.

Those three girls on Rolling Hills could ball. Seriously ball. One was their point guard, who I had to defend. Or was supposed to defend.

She schooled me all game.

The first two times down the floor, she blew right by me. The girl was even faster than Maya.

After that, I met Speedy in the backcourt because I wanted her to give up the ball so I could take her out of the offense.

At least that was the plan.

Turns out, Speedy was even better on offense when she *didn't* have the ball. She never stopped moving, she set hard screens, and she got her teammates to spots where they could do damage.

And they did.

On one play, Speedy passed the ball as she crossed mid-court and then set a pick by the three-point line. But instead of stopping, she kept going and set another screen in the low post. Then she set a third screen down low on the opposite side.

On another play, Speedy fed a teammate on the wing and then broke toward the hoop. When she couldn't get the ball back for the give-and-go, she set a screen down low for her center. He ran off the pick, got the pass, and scored the easy deuce.

That's how it went the whole game.

The game I thought we had a chance to win, we lost by twenty.

* * *

Then we lost by twenty-five to Lockport.

At halftime, we only trailed 20–16, but in the third quarter, everything Lockport threw up in the direction of the basket went in. Some of the shots were ridiculous.

Ri-dic-u-lous.

A three-pointer from beyond the top of the key that hit

the back iron, went straight up into the air, and dropped through the hoop. A jumper from the elbow that toilet-bowled the rim five times before going in. A give-and-go alley-oop where one girl threw the ball and another girl caught it in midair and then shot it before she came down.

Then with two seconds left in the quarter, the girl who threw the alley-oop heaved a shot from a step behind half-court.

Swish.

Ri-dic-u-lous.

Testing the Limits

"Something's up with Mr. Acevedo," Red said.

"What makes you say that?"

We were walking down Niagara Drive on our way to school. I was wearing my Dr. Poo-Poo costume.

Today was presentation day.

"Something's up, Mason Irving."

"He seemed fine to me."

During yesterday's game, the whole time it was raining buckets for Lockport, Coach Acevedo was clapping and cheering and pumping his fists.

But the thing is, when Red says something's up with someone, something is almost always up. One time, he did the something's-up thing with Suzanne, and the next day, she came down with the flu and was laid up for a week. Another time, he did the something's-up thing with my mom, and later that night, she told me how she had to fire three teachers. Last spring, he did the something's-up thing with Ms. Darling, and as it turns out, she was waiting to hear from her daughter, who was about to give birth.

Mr. Acevedo hadn't been in school the last two days because of the teacher workshops. We'd only seen him at the games. But he seemed exactly the same to me . . . not that I'd noticed when something was up with the others.

"Something's up, Mason Irving."

* * *

Something was up with Mr. Acevedo.

Walking into Room 208 on presentation day, I expected to see stage lights, theater curtains, and a television studio or a movie set projected on the board. I also expected to see Mr. Acevedo wearing a tuxedo or dressed like an usher or a film director.

But no. None of that.

I checked the board:

I'll explain everything once everyone is here.

Mr. Acevedo was at his desk. He wasn't reading a book. He wasn't wearing his sign. He didn't have his legs propped up. He just sat there looking like . . . looking like an ordinary teacher.

Ms. Yvonne was in the room, too, like she always was now during ELA. She sat on a rolling chair next to Red's seat with a stack of folders in her lap. For the last two days, while Mr. Acevedo was out, Red had gone with Ms. Yvonne. Red always went with Ms. Yvonne when the teacher was absent.

"You okay?" I asked Red.

He nodded. "Thanks, Mason Irving."

We headed in and sat down.

Grace walked in holding a cardboard cutout of a Fathead-size ear. Hunter and Attie arrived together—he had a saxophone and a flute, she had drumsticks and a small keyboard. Danny came in with a ginormous bowl of restaurant mints. That was his and Diego's topic: restaurant mints. Melissa wheeled

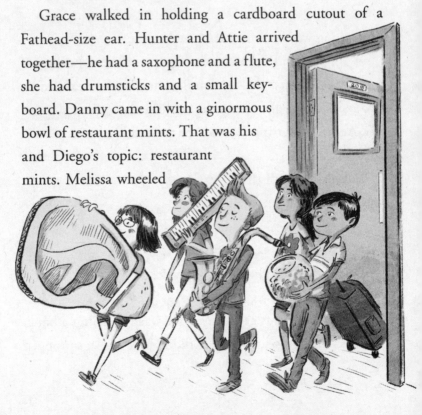

in a large rolling suitcase. X walked in wearing a 1960s wig and carrying a naked mannequin under his arm like a football.

Everyone paused by the door.

Red was right.

Something was up with Mr. Acevedo.

"Spill it, Teach," Declan said. "What's going on?"

We all sat in the meeting area. I was on a beanbag in front of the couch. Red sat on the lip of the bathtub next to X. Mr. Acevedo was in his spot.

"Let's hear it, Mr. A.," Zachary said. "What's the deal?"

Mr. Acevedo glanced at Ms. Yvonne in her rolling chair by the door and pulled back his hair. *"Nunca digas de esa agua no beberé."*

"Never say don't drink that water," Danny translated. "What's that?"

"Never say from that water I will never drink." Mr. Acevedo spoke softly.

"What does it mean?" Trinity asked.

"It means don't say you'll never do something because someday you may have to do it." He pulled back his hair again. "That's the position I'm in."

"Spill it, Teach," Declan said again. "What's up?"

"It's so disrespectful." Mr. Acevedo shook his head. "But it's out of my hands." He pulled out a booklet from underneath his iPad. "We have to postpone the presentations again until next Wednesday."

"Is that what I think it is?" Mariam asked, motioning to the booklet.

"It is," Mr. Acevedo said. "We have to take an ELA benchmark in here on Monday. All the fifth graders in the district are taking it. I just spent the last two days learning all about how to administer a test, report the data, and interpret the results. Fun times. Then yesterday afternoon, I got the e-mail about the benchmark."

He got the e-mail during the game. That's exactly what happened. Red picked up on it.

"But we haven't done any test prep," Attie said.

"I knew this was going to happen." Avery slapped her armrest. "I tried to tell you, but you wouldn't listen. Once they get our scores, they're—"

"Whoa, whoa, whoa," Mr. Acevedo interrupted. "Hold on. Attie, Ms. Goodman, stop." He rolled up the booklet. "We're not freaking out in here over this. You're going to do fine. I guarantee it."

"Just like you guaranteed we'd win a game this season," I said.

The words came out on their own. I wished them back the moment they left my lips.

"My bad." I swallowed.

"It's all good, Rip," Mr. Acevedo said. He gripped the booklet with both hands. "For the next few days, I'm expected to review with you, and it's probably in my best interest to do so."

"Your best interest?" X said.

"My best interest, X," Mr. Acevedo said. He glanced at Ms. Yvonne. "Apparently, I'm still *neglecting* my teacher duties. I'm still not being a good little soldier." He waved the booklet. "The changes I started making in here after Back-to-School Night weren't even close to being sufficient. I wasn't even close to being on the same page as outside forces." He chuckled. "Some of your parents—how should I put this—some of your parents like to be involved. Very involved. They take a hands-on approach to what goes on in school."

"Whose parents?" Grace asked.

Mr. Acevedo shook his head. "Apparently, I'm required to have you answer questions in these every day." He patted the cover of the booklet. "Then I'm required to administer practice assessments every Friday. Then I'm required to submit biweekly progress reports for each of you, reports that identify the skills you're performing above grade level, at grade level, or below grade level."

"What does all that mean?" Grace asked.

Mr. Acevedo chuckled. "It means if teachers are required

to do all that, then there's absolutely no time to teach. Which is why once we get past this silliness—and it is silliness—we're going right back to doing what we've been doing and . . ."

He flung the booklet toward the closet.

"No." Mr. Acevedo stood up. "I'm not doing this to you. No way." He drew a circle in the air with his finger. "You came in here today excited for school, and I'm not taking that away. Not like . . ." Again he pulled back his hair and looked over at Ms. Yvonne. "We'll review—or pretend to review—today, tomorrow, and Friday, but before we start down that road, we're seeing a few presentations. I *need* to see a few presentations. Who wants to be my first victim?"

Hands went up. Many hands.

But before Mr. Acevedo could pick someone, Avery was rolling to the front of Room 208.

We were presenting.

The Nasty Nine

"So our presentation is called 'Tired,' " I said.

Avery and I stood in front of Room 208 dressed as Dr. Icky-Icky and Dr. Poo-Poo. We both wore the oversize white lab coats Suzanne had gotten for us from her pharmacist friend at the hospital. There were name tags pinned to our lapels, name tags that Avery designed. We both wore large thick glasses (mine were from my second grade Harry Potter Halloween costume) and held clipboards that had the script for our presentation. I also had a metal yardstick.

"It's called 'Tired' because of these," Avery said.

I touched each of her tires with the yardstick.

Using the remote, she pressed Play.

The word *TIRED* appeared on the board. Then slowly, a wheelchair rolled across and bumped into the word, knocking it higher.

Avery's a whiz. Editing, transitions, graphics, effects—she can do it all.

Avery put together the computer presentation.

I wrote the script.

Showtime:

(*The words* Nasty Nine *appear on the board.*)

Dr. Poo-Poo: The Nasty Nine? What's the Nasty Nine, Dr. Icky-Icky?

Dr. Icky-Icky: I'm glad you asked, Dr. Poo-Poo. The Nasty Nine has to do with my tires. My tires are magnets.

Dr. Poo-Poo: Magnets?

Dr. Icky-Icky: Magnets. They attract everything. Everything sticks to them.

Dr. Poo-Poo: I know exactly what you mean.

Dr. Icky-Icky: Really, Dr. Poo-Poo? You know exactly what I mean? You know what it's like to get mud stuck in your tires? *(Scrolling images of trucks driving through mud, Woodstock 1969, Spartan races, mud wrestling)*

Dr. Poo-Poo: Stepping in mud is the worst. I have to pick it out of my sneakers with a popsicle stick. My mom bugs out when I track up the house.

Dr. Icky-Icky: You still live with your mom, Dr. Poo-Poo? Sad. Just plain sad. *(Roll neck, wag finger)* At least you can take off your shoes, Dr. Poo-Poo. I don't exactly ride around with spare tires.

Dr. Poo-Poo: Stepping in gum is even worse. *(Blow bubble, spit gum out)* It takes forever to get it all out. Other things stick to it.

Dr. Icky-Icky: Did you not hear what I said,

Dr. Poo-Poo? Were you not listening? *(Roll neck, wag finger)* You can take off your sneakers, Dr. Poo-Poo. You can put on another pair. I don't push around with spare tires, and when I get gum in my tires, it also gets in my hair. *(Flip hair)*

Dr. Poo-Poo: When I got gum in my locks, my mom bugged out. She had to redo my hair.

Dr. Icky-Icky: Your mom still does your hair, Dr. Poo-Poo? Sad. Just plain sad.

Dr. Poo-Poo: You know what's even worse than mud and gum?

Dr. Icky-Icky: Yes.

Dr. Poo-Poo: You do?

Dr. Icky-Icky: Of course I do, Dr. Poo-Poo.

Dr. Poo-Poo: Stepping in poop is the worst. *(Scrolling images of dogs pooping, horses pooping, pigeons pooping, elephants pooping)*

Dr. Icky-Icky: Try wheeling through it. No matter how hard you try, you never get it all out. It smells terrible everywhere you go.

Dr. Poo-Poo: *(Scratch head)* I'm beginning to think wheeling through nasty things may be worse than stepping in them.

Dr. Icky-Icky: You think?

Dr. Poo-Poo: I do.

Dr. Icky-Icky: You still haven't even heard the Nasty Nine.

Dr. Poo-Poo: I haven't?

Dr. Icky-Icky: You haven't. Except for poop. Poop makes the Nasty Nine.

Dr. Poo-Poo: What is the Nasty Nine?

Dr. Icky-Icky: The Nasty Nine are the nine grossest, most disgusting things that get in my tires. You want to hear what they are?

Dr. Poo-Poo: I do.

Dr. Icky-Icky: Step aside, Dr. Poo-Poo. Watch and try not to puke.

(Move to side. Play presentation)

You know how on *SportsCenter* they count down the top plays? Well, that's what we did for our Nasty Nine.

"Nine!" I shouted.

Avery—Dr. Icky-Icky—read it. "The School Cafeteria: Or as I like to call it, the obstacle course. Do you have any idea what kids drop on the floor? Do you have any idea what I have to push through? Peanut butter and jelly sandwiches, Tater Tots, applesauce, and worst of all, spilled milk. Whoever said 'Don't cry over spilled milk' never had to wheel through it."

"Eight!" everyone shouted with me.

"Winter: My least favorite season. Every trip outdoors is an adventure. Slush puddles are always deeper than you think. Always. Sand and salt always get stuck in your tread. Always. When you bring sand and salt indoors, it always scratches the floors. Always. The most important thing about winter—whatever you do, avoid yellow snow."

"Seven!"

"Movie Theaters: Sticky soda is everywhere. Sticky popcorn butter is everywhere. Don't believe me? The next time you go to the movies, put your palm on the floor. That's what I'm parked in."

"Six!"

"School Bathrooms: You think walking in the school bathroom is gross? Try rolling through it. Getting toilet paper stuck to my tires is the least of my worries. Just check out the color of the tiles by the toilets. There's a reason I never go in there without my canister of disinfecting wipes."

"Five!"

"Tar: On hot summer days when I'm in the city, I don't cross the street. Why? Tar melts. That means the city street melts. That means the city street sticks to my tires. That means everything sticks to my tires. That means I'm a hot mess."

"Four!"

"Poop and Crap: Poop and crap, poop and crap, poop and crap, poop and crap. It's everywhere, and until you're a wheeler, you have no clue how everywhere it is. People don't pick up after their dogs. Bird droppings are all over. But nothing—absolutely nothing—compares to human baby poop. Trust me on this one, it's worse than all other poop put together."

"Three!"

"The Dead: We live among the dead. Sidewalks are cemeteries. Worms, especially on rainy days. Cockroaches, especially when it's dark. Baby birds, especially in the spring. Yes, baby birds. Baby bird guts, baby bird heads. Chew on that."

"Two!"

"Gas Stations: I never get out of the car at a gas station. Never. Why? One time, I pushed through oil and gasoline. That was all it took. One time. When I got back in the car, the car reeked. When I got home, the house reeked. For days. No, I never get out of the car at gas stations. Never."

"One!"

"Glass: Why is glass number one? Not because of flat tires. Not because it gets stuck in the tread and scratches everything. But because when it gets stuck in the tread and I don't know it's there, I slice open my hand. Trust me, when there's a deep cut across your palm, it's impossible to push a wheelchair."

The word *TIRED* appeared on the board again. Then our names faded. Just like that, we were done. We were finished with the project.

We did it.

As I started back to my desk, the most amazing thing of all happened: everyone in Room 208 stood and cheered.

"Way to go, Mason Irving!" Red raced up, hands raised.

We broke out our handshake: "High-five, high-five. Elbow, elbow," we chanted. "Right, right. Left, left. Fist, fist, knuckles, blow it up. Turn, jump, bump . . ."

"Boo-yah!" the whole class shouted.

Red spun to Avery. "Way to go, Avery Goodman," he said. He hugged her.

I held out my fist.

She gave me a pound. "Way to go, dude."

Rematch

Everyone's parents were here for the rematch against Millwood, but they weren't on the stage like for the game against Voigt. They were on the sideline across from our bench.

Millwood's fans had the stage. Millwood's fans *filled* the stage. Millwood had something to play for. After they beat us last time, they had lost a second game. Today they needed a win to qualify for the playoffs.

That's what Coach Crazy was yelling about: "This is a playoff game!" he shouted. "We need today. We're taking it to this team. Just like last time. As soon as that ball goes up . . ."

With my basketball eyes, I spotted Avery wheeling into the gym. A second later, Red saw her, too.

"Avery Goodman!" He waved. "Avery Goodman's here."

She didn't park next to the parents. Instead, she rolled across the court to our bench.

"This is for players only," I said. "You can't be here." I pointed to the far sideline. "Our fans sit—"

"Fans?" Avery laughed. "Dude, those aren't fans. Those are parents. You have one fan here, and your one fan is watching her first basketball game from right here."

I knew better than to argue.

Across the gym, Suzanne and my mom stood by the door. Suzanne had to be here today. If Red was going to be on the bench down the sideline from Coach Crazy, Coach Acevedo insisted she be here.

I checked Red. His earplugs were in. His back was to Coach Crazy.

"Let's bring it in, United," Coach Acevedo said.

We hustled into a huddle in front of our bench.

"Excellent to see you here, Avery," Coach Acevedo said. "We could use a good-luck charm today." He winked at Red standing behind her and then thumbed the court. "I don't have to tell you who we're up against today, but we play the game because anything's possible. Anything. And I have a good feeling about today."

"I have a good feeling about today, too, Coach Acevedo," Red said.

"Every team needs a Blake Daniels." Coach Acevedo slide-stepped to Red, gave him a quick pound, and then hopped back to the middle. "That's our attitude today.

That's our body language. That's how we play." He patted his chest. "We play like we all have a good feeling about today." He checked the iPad. "Rip, Keith, Wil, Maya, Jason—you're our first five."

"Let's do this," Keith said. He held out his fist.

I gave him a pound.

"Hands in, Clifton United," Coach Acevedo said.

He waited for every hand.

"On three," he said, "we say 'team.' One, two, three . . ."

"Team!"

* * *

Millwood's Mega-Man batted the opening tip out of bounds, so we got the ball first. I took the inbounds from Maya in the backcourt. I expected a suffocating, full-court press, but no. My man hung back by the three-point circle. I crossed half-court, faked to Wil, and then hit Keith with a pass as he rolled off Maya's pick.

Stop. Set. Pop. Shoot.

Swish!

"Clifton United's winning!" Red shouted. "Go, Keith Krebs!"

I turned to sprint back on defense, but before my first foot landed, I spotted the inbounds pass. A lazy, lollipop pass. I changed direction, Rip Hamilton–style, plucked the ball out of the air, and shot the layup.

Swish!

"Go, Clifton United!" a few parents cheered.

"Great hustle, number thirty-two," shouted Keith's dad.

Coach Crazy was shouting, too.

"What kind of pass was that? What are you doing out there? Use your heads." He jabbed his fingers into his temple. "How could you let that gnat steal the ball?"

Gnat.

Coach Crazy called me Gnat. It was the first time all season anyone had called me Gnat.

Millwood was careful inbounding the ball this time, but I still acted the gnat in their backcourt. It took them four passes to get over half-court.

My man had the ball in the frontcourt. With my basketball eyes, I checked Maya on my right. Suddenly, she bolted from her man, and we swarmed the point guard, four arms waving. He tried dribbling through us, but instead, he dribbled off his knee.

Tweet!

"Blue ball going down," the ref called.

Maya scooped up the rock, flipped it to the ref, and then raced out of bounds.

"Ball's in." The ref handed the ball to Maya.

She whipped it inbounds and hit Keith streaking down the court.

A breakaway layup.

"Time-out!" Coach Crazy exploded. "Time-out!"

Tweet!

"Time-out, Orange." The ref pointed to the Millwood bench.

Coach Acevedo charged onto the court.

"That's how we get things going!" He gave pounds all around. "That's how we're playing today. We're keeping this body language all game." He turned to me. "Rip, heads-up basketball out there. Way to catch them sleeping. Maya and Keith—great pass, great finish. That was a thing of beauty." He clapped hard. "Let's keep playing Clifton United basketball."

* * *

We kept playing Clifton United basketball, and at the end of the first, we led by ten.

But in the second, Millwood chipped away at our lead, and by late in the quarter, they trimmed it to two. With eight seconds left, I drew a foul and sank both ends of a one-and-one.

At the half, we led 24–20.

"Get ready for them to start using their bodies," Coach Acevedo said at halftime.

"They aren't already?" Keith said.

"That big kid with the glasses needs to cut his nails," Emily added. She held out her arm, which was covered in scratches.

"They're going to get even more physical," Coach Acevedo said. "When they do, we don't get caught up in it. We keep our body language. We keep playing like we have a good feeling about today. We keep playing Clifton United basketball."

* * *

In the third quarter, Millwood came out on fire. They scored the first eight points and jumped in front, 28–24.

"Take it to them!" Coach Crazy shouted. "Take it to them!"

Their fans were raging, too.

"Mill-wood!" they cheered and clapped every time they had the ball. "Mill-wood!"

"Dee-fense!" they cheered and clapped every time we had the ball. "Dee-fense!"

Now at any other point this season, I would've said we were done. No way were we digging ourselves out of this hole.

But not today.

Today, that doubt didn't creep in. Not even for less than a nanosecond. Not only was I playing like I had a good feeling about today, I *did* have a good feeling about today.

Midway through the third, Coach Acevedo brought in Mehdi, Emily, and Jeffrey. It was the burst of energy off the bench that we needed. They played in-your-grille defense and outmuscled Millwood's monsters under the boards.

Then Keith got hot, blistering hot: A jumper from the

corner. A three-pointer from the top of the key. A running one-hander across the lane.

Our parents erupted:

"Keith Krebs!" they cheered. "Keith Krebs!"

Everyone on our bench—Avery included—waved towels and banged chairs.

Heading to the final quarter: Millwood 37, Clifton 36.

* * *

"We're throwing a curve to start the fourth," Coach Acevedo said in the huddle. "We're going small. Rip, Mikey, Maya, Keith, Wil—you're our five." He drew a circle in the air. "I want everyone running around like Rip out there. Make them chase after you. We're going to beat them with speed and mismatches. Let's go, hands in."

He waited for every hand.

"On three, 'team.' One, two, three . . ."

"Team!"

* * *

On the opening play, we whipped that ball around. Millwood's monsters tried to keep up with our passing, but they couldn't. When the rock came back to me for the *third* time, I fired from the elbow.

Swish!

"Clifton takes the lead!" Red leaped off his chair. "Way to go, Mason Irving!"

"Dee-fense!" our parents cheered.

"Dee-fense!" Our bench pounded the floor.

But Millwood answered right back. They buried a jumper and retook the lead.

That's how it went all quarter long:

Back and forth.

Back and forth.

With twenty-three seconds left, we clung to a one-point lead.

My man had the ball. He brought the ball upcourt and looked inside, but no way was I letting him make that pass. So he fed Super-Size on the wing. Super-Size took the shot.

Swish.

"Time-out!" we all shouted.

Tweet!

"Time-out, Blue!" the ref called.

Eleven seconds to go.

"Plenty of time," Coach Acevedo said, dropping to a knee in the center of our huddle. "Eleven seconds is plenty of time." He tapped my high-tops. "Rip, you're taking the ball out under the basket. Here's what we're running."

Coach Acevedo diagrammed the play and held up the screen. I needed to get the ball to Jason between half-court and the top of the key. Once Jason had the ball, he had two options—hit Maya in the corner or find Keith cutting toward the hoop on the far side.

"You played your hearts out this afternoon," Coach Acevedo said after going over everyone's assignments. "I am so proud of all of you. This is what it means to be a team. On three, 'team.' One, two, three . . ."

"Team!"

* * *

Jason, Mehdi, Keith, Maya, and I took the floor.

On the bench, Clifton United linked arms.

"U-ni-ted!" our parents cheered. "U-ni-ted!"

"Dee-fense!" the Millwood fans screamed. "Dee-fense!"

Coach Acevedo pointed to Keith and waved him closer to the three-point circle. He motioned for Jason to hold his spot.

"Three feet," the ref said to the Millwood player defending me. He waited for the player to take a half-step back and then handed me the ball. "Ball's in."

I bolted down the end line. Since I was taking the ball out after a basket, I was allowed to run out of bounds. But Millwood's defender didn't know I could. It bought me the space I needed. I fired a baseball pass to Jason. He caught the ball over his head, turned toward the hoop, and looked to Maya. Maya ran off Mehdi's screen, but she couldn't shake her man. So Jason pivoted to Keith. Keith had a step on his defender, so Jason led him with a pass.

"Go! Go!" Coach Acevedo waved. "Five seconds!"

Lowering his shoulder, Keith dribbled across the three-point arc and headed for the hoop. As he left his feet, Mega-Man shifted over and leaped into the air.

The two collided.

Mega-Man's elbow whacked Keith in the head.

Tweet! Tweet!

"Good if it goes!" the referee called. He raised his arm.

The buzzer sounded.

Keith crumpled to the floor.

The shot hit the side of the backboard and bounded away.

"Foul's on number thirty-three, Orange," the referee said, pointing at Mega-Man. "Blue is shooting two." He held up two fingers and faced the coaches. "Let's have all players off the floor. There's no time remaining. Only the shooter . . ."

Under the hoop, as Keith sat up, blood poured over his fingers, which were covering his eye.

"Can I get some towels here?" The referee raced over. "Hold still, son." He gripped Keith's shoulder.

Coach Acevedo charged onto the court. So did Keith's mom and dad. So did Suzanne. Within a few seconds, Suzanne was holding a towel over Keith's eye as they all walked Keith to the boys' bathroom.

Coach Acevedo came back out a moment later.

"Keith's okay," he said, jogging to our bench. "He has a cut over his eye, but it looks worse than it is. Heads bleed a lot." He held up a finger. "Give me a sec. I need to talk to the ref and find out the situation. Keith's out of the game."

Keith's out of the game.

I knew the situation. I knew the rule. If a player was unable to shoot free throws because of an injury, the opposing coach was allowed to choose any player to shoot the free throws.

Any player.

The ref, Coach Acevedo, and Coach Crazy stood at center court. I couldn't hear what they were saying, but I knew exactly what they were saying.

Then Coach Acevedo trotted our way.

"Rip," he said, waving me up.

I hustled to him.

"I need you to talk to Red," he said. "Their coach is allowed to choose anyone from our bench to shoot the free throws. He's choosing Red."

"Red's not allowed to play. Suzanne—"

"I know," he cut me off. "I said something to her in the locker room. I had a feeling this would happen. She understands the situation." He pulled back his hair. "He knows exactly what he's doing. It's a terrible thing."

"You should tell Red he's in," I said.

"I think it would be better coming from you."

I shook my head. "You should tell him."

Coach Acevedo paused. "Okay. But I want you standing right next to me when I do."

We headed for Red.

"Are your earplugs in?" Coach Acevedo asked, walking up.

Red pressed a finger to each ear. "They are, Coach Acevedo."

"Good." He nodded to the court. "You're in the game, Red."

"Me?" Red pointed to his number and then looked at me.

"You," Coach Acevedo said. "You're in for Keith."

"I'm playing?" Red hunched his shoulders.

"You're playing," I said, nodding. "You can do it."

"I don't know, Mason Irving." Red started to sway.

Old-man face.

"You can do it, Red."

"I don't know."

"I do!"

We all turned.

Avery rolled up and hockey-stopped beside me.

"You can do it, Red," she said. "I know you can."

"You're shooting Keith's free throws," Coach Acevedo said.

"Free throws." Red stopped swaying. "Really?"

"Really. Their coach is allowed to pick anyone to shoot the free throws. He's picking you."

"I'm shooting free throws in a game?" Red basketball-smiled. "My mom said I could?" He hopped from foot to foot.

"She did."

"Did you hear that, Mason Irving?" Red's basketball grin grew as wide as I'd ever seen it. "I'm shooting Keith Krebs's free throws. I'm shooting free throws in a game."

"You ready?" I said.

"Oh, yeah! Ready as I'll ever be, Mason Irving."

I patted his chest. "Their fans are going to get loud."

"I'm shooting Keith Krebs's free throws," he said again, hopping faster.

"Don't listen to their fans," Avery said. "No matter what they say, don't listen."

"You sure you're up for this, Red?" Coach Acevedo said. "You don't have to—"

"I'm your free-throw-shooting machine, Coach Acevedo."

"You sure are." He shook Red's hair. It was the first time I'd ever seen Red let anyone touch his hair that way. "Every team needs a Blake Daniels."

"Handshake for good luck?" I said.

"Handshake for good luck!"

We went right into it: "High-five, high-five. Elbow, elbow. Right, right. Left, left. Fist, fist, knuckles, blow it up. Turn, jump, bump . . ."

"Boo-yah!" everyone on Clifton United cheered.

Red pressed his earplugs and then bounded for the scorer's table.

"Blake Daniels, number twenty-four, checking in."

The referee smiled and pointed to the court.

Red took the floor.

By himself.

I checked the gym. Down the court, Coach Crazy was smiling, laughing. On the stage, all the Millwood fans were standing and shouting and waving their arms.

I clasped my hands and pressed my thumb and knuckles to my lips.

C'mon, Red. You got this. Make it. Make it. Make it.

"You can do it, Red!" Avery sat on the edge of her chair and gripped her brakes. "You got this, dude."

"Go, number twenty-four!" Suzanne shouted. She was back on the sidelines with the parents. "Go, Red!"

All Clifton United—including Coach Acevedo—joined arms.

Red was locked in.

"Two shots," the ref said, handing him the ball. "Good luck, son."

"Thanks, Mr. Referee."

Red dropped the ball and trapped it underfoot soccer-style. He placed a finger over each ear and took several breaths. He picked up the ball with both hands, squared his shoulders, and stared at the front rim. Then he dribbled the ball three quick times low to the ground and stood back up. He rotated the ball until his fingers gripped it around the word SPALDING, looked at the rim again, extended his arms, and shot the ball.

Underhanded.

Swish!

Clifton 56, Millwood 56.

We leaped.

"Boo-yah!" I hammer-fisted the air.

"Dude!" Avery cheered, waving her arms.

All our parents jumped around.

The team joined arms again. I joined one arm in Alex's, the other in Avery's.

"One shot," the referee said, smiling. He handed the basketball to Red. "Good luck, son."

"Thanks, Mr. Referee."

Red dropped the ball and trapped it soccer-style under his foot.

"It all comes down to this," I play-by-played softly. "No time on the clock. Knotted at fifty-six. Clifton United's free-throw-shooting machine is on the line. He takes his dribbles, spins the ball, and stares at the rim. For the W. For Clifton United's first win of the season. The underhanded free throw . . ."

Swish!

"It's good! It's good!" I announced. "Clifton United has pulled off the upset of the year. Clifton 57, Millwood 56. Go crazy, folks! Go crazy!"

We stormed the court.

The Benchmark

"Good luck," Mr. Acevedo said. "You may begin."

You may begin.

As soon as a teacher says those three words at the start of a test, I begin to sweat and shake and bug out. Then when I try to read the first question, the information bounces off my brain. It's as if my brain suddenly turns into one of those nonstick pots my mom cooks with. Then I start to sweat and shake and bug even more because I'm losing time. When I'm finally able to focus, I have to read even slower than usual because that's the only way the information sticks, but because I'm reading in super slow-mo, I'm buggin' even more because I'm wasting even more time.

Not today.

Today, I went with Mr. Acevedo's suggestion. When he said, "You may begin," I put down my pencil.

I let out a puff and checked the room. Room 208 didn't look like Room 208: All the walls were covered with brown paper. The couch, bathtub, and beanbags were pushed against the cubbies. Mr. Acevedo's desk was in front by the board. Our desks were in rows.

I sat at the desk in back of Grace and in front of Lana, the one with the notecard with my name on it taped to the front. Avery sat by the windows, near where Red usually sits. Red was off with Ms. Yvonne.

I let out another puff, picked up my pencil, and scanned the test. The first part was the editing part. I couldn't believe my eyes. There was only one question: A concerned citizen had written a letter to the editor of a newspaper requesting that a stop sign be installed at a busy intersection. The letter was filled with errors. We had to correct it and rewrite it.

That was it.

* * *

The second part of the benchmark was the listening part.

Mr. Acevedo read us a passage. Twice. He read like he read during T3.

It was a story about a family sitting around a breakfast table preparing for a big day. But the story didn't say what the big day was.

When he finished reading, I *scanned* the questions:

- *How does the setting . . .*
- *When the grandmother's character . . .*
- *What predictions can you make based on . . .*
- *Which character best . . .*
- *How does the mood of the passage change from . . .*
- *Where is the family . . .*

Every question stuck to my brain like glue.

We took the third part of the benchmark—the writing part—in the afternoon.

"There's only one question," Mr. Acevedo said. "You have plenty of time. You're going to do great. I guarantee it. You may begin."

I put down my pencil and scanned the question:

> *Describe a situation in which you have been asked to do something you didn't want to do. Your response should include the following: A detailed description of the situation. A detailed explanation of why you didn't want to do the requested task. A detailed explanation of the*

*process. A detailed explanation of the results of
the process.*

Under the desk, I pumped my fist. It was as if the question didn't say, *Describe a situation in which you have been asked to do something you didn't want to do,* but rather, *Describe your experience working on the "That's Nasty" project.*

I had this one, too.

Guaranteed

The next morning, I met Red at the end of his driveway at 7:25, and we walked our usual route to RJE. At the schoolyard, I tossed my bag over the fence, and he caught it by the straps.

We zigzagged through the portables, shared the oatmeal-raisin granola bar, and headed for the playground. We obstacle-coursed the jungle gym, tapped our wooden posts, and headed for the front entrance, turning onto the circular driveway sidewalk just as the first buses . . .

I stopped dead in my tracks.

Avery and Mr. Acevedo were by the front doors.

"Let's go have a conversation," Mr. Acevedo said, smiling. He gave Red a pound. "Let's head to the Amp."

* * *

"Let me start with you, Red," Mr. Acevedo said.

He sat cross-legged on the end of the front-row bench

with a folder on his lap. Avery sat beside him. Red and I sat in the second row facing him.

"Ms. Yvonne said that was the first time you took one of those without extended time."

"Yes, Mr. Acevedo."

"I don't have your results yet, but Ms. Yvonne said that was the best you ever did. By far."

"Bam!" Red raised his arms.

Mr. Acevedo turned to Avery. "Same thing goes for you, Ms. Goodman."

"Don't play, Mr. Acevedo," she said.

"I'm not playing. I have your results." He tapped the folder. "Let's talk about the writing portion first. What did you write about?"

"Working with Rip," she said.

"Seriously?" I said.

"You two haven't talked about this yet?" Mr. Acevedo opened the folder.

We both shook our heads.

"You wrote about each other. She wrote about working with you. You wrote about working with her."

I twisted a lock by my forehead and smiled.

"That was the best I ever did in writing?" Avery asked.

"Not just writing, Ms. Goodman. Editing, listening, *and* writing.

"That goes for both of you. In fact, every student in Room 208 showed improvement."

"Just like you guaranteed."

I sprang to my feet and spun to Red. "Handshake!"

Red leaped into it.

"High-five, high-five. Elbow, elbow," we cheered together. "Right, right. Left, left. Fist, fist, knuckles, blow it up. Turn, jump, bump . . ."

"Boo-yah!"
the four of us
shouted.

Acknowledgments

I loved every part of working on this book. Except for this part. I avoided writing these acknowledgments for as long as I possibly could. Why? I know I'm going to leave someone out. It will hit me as soon as I see this in print.

With that said, thanks and love to . . .

Erin Murphy, my agent. I'm listening to the music of the moment. Our name is our virtue.

Wes Adams, my editor. You pushed me as a writer like no one before. You challenged me on every page. Boo-yah!

Farrar Straus Giroux and the whole Macmillan Children's Publishing Group. You rallied behind this project. You poured your hearts into this project. You are this project.

Illustrator Tim Probert, whose pictures capture the energy and essence of the story.

Elizabeth Acevedo, my student, my friend. Whenever I visit schools, I'm often asked what inspires me. I always talk about the relentless passion of Elizabeth Acevedo.

Eva Ruiz, my Spanish expert and supernova friend who dreams in larger-than-life.

Anna Rekate, the best educator I've ever worked for. Your values and vision belong in every school around the globe. You're getting there.

Yvonne Salgado, the best educator I ever worked with. Empathy comes first. You modeled that every day in our classroom.

Owa Brandstein, my basketball guru, who made sure my hoops sequences were close enough to real and who puts up with my borderline-delusional Brooklyn Nets fandom.

Teddy Bailey and Evan Bailey, my gamer gurus, who made sure I didn't embarrass myself too much writing video-game scenes.

Helen Leonard, founder of the Paragon School in Orlando, Florida, who gave me the strength and tools to develop the character of Rip. Every student matters.

Christine Carter, Julia Garstecki, Jane Jergensen, and Jennifer Lucas, who read through early drafts, answered all my questions, and reinforced the notion that every student matters.

April Coughlin, for spending hours and hours with me on the character of Avery. You opened my eyes.

Cree and Robin Mitchell, for embodying perseverance.

Tracey Appelbaum and Cindy Leff, who helped me design an eleven-year-old boy's bedroom.

Tony Sinanis and Ami Uselman, who helped me design Reese Jones Elementary School.

Lindsay Jones, who gave the world the beautiful Reese.

Jackie Woodson, for sitting with me at DuJour and explaining the finer points of black hair care, and for sitting with my sixth graders on the auditorium stage at the West Farms School in the Tremont section of the Bronx way back in nineteen ninety-something and discussing Mel, Sean, Ralph, and Angie.

Stephanie Lurie and Kareem Abdul-Jabbar, who gave me the kick in the butt I didn't know I needed to write this book.

Kate Messner, your *Real Revision* should be on every writer's bookshelf. Wendy Mass, your contribution to *Real Revision* should be used by every writing teacher.

Kevin and Katniss, my family. Thank you for the constant distractions. Thank you for your patience and kindness. Thank you for the love.

—P.B.

GOFISH

PHIL BILDNER

What did you want to be when you grew up?
I wanted to be a basketball player or baseball player, but size and ability got in the way. I guess I wanted to be a lawyer because that's what the people in my life told me I wanted to be. Fortunately, I realized I had to be what *I* wanted to be.

When did you realize you wanted to be a writer?
I always loved to write, but I never considered it for a career until I was teaching middle school in the New York City public schools. My students and experiences there inspired me to write.

What's your favorite childhood memory?
Going to ball games! I loved going to Shea Stadium to watch the New York Mets, Nassau Coliseum to watch the New York Islanders, and Madison Square Garden to watch the New York Knicks.

As a young person, who did you look up to most?
I don't know if there was one person in particular that I looked up to. Of course, I had favorite athletes, musicians, and statesmen, but I don't think there was any one individual or hero that I aspired to be like more than anyone else.

What was your favorite thing about school?

In fifth grade, my teacher was Mr. Kramer. He was my first male teacher, and he ran his classroom in an unconventional manner. More than any other teacher, he made school and learning fun.

What were your hobbies as a kid? What are your hobbies now?

As a kid, I loved playing ball and playing with my dogs. I would also spend hours on my bedroom floor playing Strat-O-Matic Baseball, the pre-cursor to fantasy baseball. My hobbies now include reading, hiking, working out, and traveling. I still love playing ball and playing with my dog (obviously, it's a different dog).

Did you play sports as a kid?

I did! I played baseball, basketball, and soccer. I always wanted to be outside running around. No matter where I went, I always looked for a pick-up game of hoops.

What was your first job, and what was your "worst" job?

My first job was shoveling snow. My friend Steven and I would go around and knock on doors every time it snowed. Easy money and all cash! My worst job was when I worked at Wendy's with my friend Mitchell. We lasted two nights. Then we got a job packing bicycles and bicycle parts in a warehouse . . . which really wasn't all that much better.

What book is on your nightstand now?

It's rare that I get to read a book more than once, but right now, I'm re-reading (for the third time) Ta-Nehisi Coates's *Between the World and Me*. It's incredibly powerful and relevant. It's one of those books that will end up on high school reading lists for years to come.

How did you celebrate publishing your first book?
My first book was *Shoeless Joe & Black Betsy*. We had a publication party at Books of Wonder, a bookstore in New York City. At the time, I was still teaching middle school. Many of my students and their families attended. It was pretty special.

Where do you write your books?
All different places! I take a writer's notebook with me wherever I go. When I lived in the city, I would write on the subway all the time. I also enjoyed writing on the roof of my apartment building. Nowadays, most of my writing takes place either in my office at home or on my back porch. When I'm on the road, you'll find me writing on airplanes and in my hotel room. I guess I can write pretty much anywhere!

What sparked your imagination for the Rip and Red series?
When I visit schools, I always tell kids to write about what you know and love. I taught middle school for many years. I played basketball for many years. Nowadays, I visit schools around the world and interact with kids and educators in ways I never imagined. My life experiences—past and current—inspired me to write this series.

What challenges do you face in the writing process, and how do you overcome them?
I don't have enough time to write all the things I want to write. It forces me to prioritize. For instance, as I'm answering these questions, I'm finishing up the third Rip and Red book. However, I've already got my eye on a picture book manuscript

I worked on a couple of years ago that wasn't clicking, but now I think I found the way to make it sing. I can't wait to dive back in. I also can't wait to work on an idea for an early chapter book. I need to clone myself!

What is your favorite word?
Empathy.

If you could live in any fictional world, what would it be?
The Hogwarts School of Witchcraft and Wizardry. Because it is the Hogwarts School of Witchcraft and Wizardry.

Who is your favorite fictional character?
Ignatius Reilly from John Kennedy Toole's *A Confederacy of Dunces.*

What was your favorite book when you were a kid? Do you have a favorite book now?
As a kid, I read the newspaper every morning. I would sit in the middle of the kitchen floor and devour the sports pages of *The New York Times*. I also read lots of sports biographies. Then in sixth grade, I read a book I wasn't allowed to read because it was supposedly too grown up for me. I read *Alive* by Piers Paul Read, the story of the rugby team whose plane crashed in the Andes Mountains. It was intense! My favorite book now? That's easy. All the ones I read aloud to my students are my all-time faves. Those were the best reading moments of my life.

If you could travel in time, where would you go and what would you do?
I would travel back in time and visit my teenage self and tell him to have the courage and conviction to be the person he really is.

What's the best advice you have ever received about writing?
Read. In order to write, you have to read. It doesn't matter what you're reading, so long as you're reading something.

What advice do you wish someone had given you when you were younger?
Live your life, not the life others want you to live or the life you think you're supposed to live.

Do you ever get writer's block? What do you do to get back on track?
I rarely get writer's block, but if I ever need to jump-start my writing, I usually find a different place to write. A change of scenery—more often than not—does the trick.

What do you want readers to remember about your books?
That they were able to see themselves or an aspect of themselves in the books, and as a result, they're books they want to share with others.

What would you do if you ever stopped writing?
I hope I never have to find out the real answer to that question, but if I wasn't writing, I'd be teaching in some capacity.

If you were a superhero, what would your superpower be?
Over the years, I've answered this question in many different ways. I've wanted to be able to turn invisible, time travel, shape-shift, and fly (among many others). Right now, I'm thinking I'd want a pause button—the power to stop everything so that I can do all the things I want and need to

do, and also to arrange things in the way that I want them to be.

Do you have any strange or funny habits? Did you when you were a kid?

I'll tell you about one I have now: When I lived in the city, I would sometimes go up to the rooftop of my apartment building, plug in my music, and dance like nobody's watching . . . only I know there had to be lots of people watching from other buildings and windows. I'm sure some stranger shot some vid of me doing this and posted it on YouTube. Now I do the dancing-by-myself thing in my backyard.

What do you consider to be your greatest accomplishment?

That's a tough one, but I'll go with a sports one. I ran the New York City Marathon twice. The first time I ran it, I barely even trained. At the time, I wasn't even a runner. I just played basketball and worked out. My friend had an extra number, so I ran with him. When I finished, I was tired, but I actually had a little gas left in the tank. So the next year, I trained and set an ambitious goal. I told myself if met my goal, I'd never run another marathon. I did it!

What would your readers be most surprised to learn about?

Whenever I visit schools, if kids haven't seen a picture of me or visited my website and watched my vids, they're always surprised by my appearance. They don't think I look like a writer . . . whatever a writer is supposed to look like!

There's a new girl in school.
And she's got game.

Keep reading for an excerpt.

Takara Eid

"This is Takara," Mr. Acevedo said after everyone had arrived. He stood next to her at the front of the class. "She's joining us in here. Room 208 has a new addition."

A new addition?

The fifth grade never got new students. In the lower grades, kids came and went all the time, and each grade also had three or four classes. But the fifth grade had only one class. The last time we got new kids was when the twins, Lana and Ana, moved here in second grade.

"Would you like to introduce yourself?" Mr. Acevedo asked.

"Yeppers," she said.

A couple kids snickered. Mr. Acevedo silenced them with a stare.

"I'm Takara," she said. She held up her arms and pushed her hip out to the side like a dancer at the end of a number. "Takara Eid. But everyone calls me Tiki. I'm Egyptian. Well, my pop's from Egypt." She patted her cheeks and tilted her head. "That's why I'm brown."

Welcome
to
Room
208

A lot more than a couple kids wanted to snicker—including me. But the don't-you-dare lasers shooting from Mr. Acevedo's eyes stopped us.

Tiki wore a bright yellow hoodie shirt with the Eiffel Tower on the front, purple pants like Trinity's and Attie's, and light-blue canvas low-tops with one white shoelace and one black shoelace.

"So we now have thirteen girls and thirteen boys," Melissa said.

"We do," Mr. Acevedo said.

"We've never had as many girls." She stood up, looked down at Noah sitting next to her, and smiled. "We're bigger than you, too."

The girls were bigger than the boys this year. Whenever I stood next to Melissa, Grace, or Isa, I felt like I was their little brother.

The biggest boy, Bryan, was no longer in the class. He was the biggest kid at RJE. But his family had to move. Mr. Acevedo told us about it last week during CC, Community Circle. That's our class meeting time.

"Let's see where I'm going to put you, Tiki." Mr. Acevedo brushed some hair off his face and looked around the room. "Rip and Red, there are two open seats at your table. I'm going to have her join you."

"Which one of you is Rip?" Tiki blurted loudly.

I started to reply but she cut me off.

"Gollygadzookers." She snort-laughed. She patted her cheeks again. "I can't believe I said that out loud. Of course I know which one of you is Red."

"People call me Red because of my hair," Red said. "My real name is Blake Daniels. Rip's real name is Mason Irving."

She looked right at me. "There was a kid at my old school named Rip." She pumped her eyebrows. "Everyone called him Rip because he ripped farts all the time."

Everyone laughed.

Everyone but me.

"That's not why people call me Rip," I said.

She held up her hands with her fingers spread apart. "Could you imagine if that was the reason? That would be so freakaliciously funny."

My cheeks blazed. Some people don't think black people blush or turn red, but trust me, we do.

I let out a loud puff. This was how nicknames got started. Bad nicknames. Bad nicknames that stuck. Like a fart nickname. A fart nickname the year before middle school.

"So what does . . . what does your name mean?" I asked.

"*Eid* means 'festival'!" She raised her arms again. "So if

your last name was Eid, and you farted a lot, it would be a farting festival!"

Everyone laughed again.

I didn't.

"Rip," Mr. Acevedo said, "take Tiki around today. Show her Room 208. Show her what RJE is all about."

Tiki Time

I stared at Tiki. She sat straight across from me. She and Red were chatting like besties.

"Mr. Acevedo's a big fan of breaks," Red said. "That's why we're taking one now."

"I'm a big fan of breaks, too," Tiki said, smiling.

"Breaks last about five to ten minutes," Red said.

"It would be horrible if cars and trucks didn't stop!" Tiki leaned forward. "I'm a big fan of *brakes*, too."

"Mr. Acevedo is not a big fan of homework." Red kept going. "Mr. Acevedo's not a big fan of tests."

"Something tells me Mr. Acevedo's not a big fan of worksheets either."

"Mr. Acevedo's not, Takara Eid!" Red pointed to the large NWZ—No Worksheet Zone—sign next to the white-board.

I let out a puff.

After Bryan left last week, Mr. Acevedo said everyone

could change seats, but Red and I didn't because we liked
our seats by the windows, and Red only sits facing doors.
Miles moved to a table in the back so he could sit with
Noah, and Trinity moved to the middle table with the
OMG girls—Olivia, Mariam, and Grace. That meant
the two seats across from Red and me were open. We had
the table to ourselves.

Until . . .

"Do you know what T3 is, Takara Eid?" Red asked.

"I have a hunchabalooga you're going to tell me, Blake
Daniels."

"*Hunchabalooga* isn't even a word," I said.

"It is to me." Tiki pointed to herself with both index fingers. "I love making up words."

"T3 is Teacher's Theater Time," Red said. "That's when Mr. Acevedo reads to the class. Mr. Acevedo reads to the class every day. Mr. Acevedo's the best reader."

"You can't just make up words," I said.

"Why not?" Tiki placed her elbows on the table and cupped her hands around her chin. "I love having my own words. It's so much fun. Fa-real-zees. That means for real."

"You can't do that."

"Who says?"

I twisted a lock near my forehead at its root and looked over at Mr. Acevedo. He was sitting on the lip of the bathtub in the meeting area, talking with Diego and Xander.

Why do I have to show her around? Why can't somebody else?

"At this one school I went to," Tiki said, "there were fifteen fifth-grade classes. Fifteen! And at this other school, there were only forty-four kids in the whole school."

"How many schools have you been to, Takara Eid?" Red asked.

"This year?" She counted fingers. "Four."

"Why do you move around so much?" I asked.

"We just do," she said.

"We call independent reading Choice," Red said. "We call it Choice because we're allowed to read whatever we want."

"I like reading nonfiction," Tiki said.

"Most of the nonfiction is over there." Red pointed to the corner by the Swag Wall. "Some of the nonfiction is on top of the cubbies in the silver toolboxes. Some of the non-fiction is in the orange, green, and yellow milk crates."

Ms. Yvonne walked in.

"Hi, Ms. Yvonne." Red waved.

"Hi, Red," Ms. Yvonne said, heading for our table. "And you must be Takara."

"Yeppers," she said. "Everyone calls me Tiki, except for Red."

Ms. Yvonne sat down. "Honey, why don't you put those away?" She nodded to the headphones still around Red's neck. "You don't need them now."

Red slipped them off his neck, spun them around his wrist, and rolled them into his desk. Red can do tons of cool tricks with his headphones.

"As soon as break ends," Ms. Yvonne said to Red, "we're going over your writer's notebook."

"Thanks, Ms. Yvonne."

"I want to see yours, too," she said to me.

Whenever Ms. Yvonne was in ELA—which was most of the time—she helped all the kids, not just the ones with services.

I tilted back my chair, grabbed a composition notebook from the windowsill, and slid it across to Tiki.

"Here," I said.

"All your writing work goes in there." Ms. Yvonne tapped the cover. "So you're from Egypt, Tiki?"

"My family is."

"Have you ever been?"

"Not yet." Her thick eyebrows curved up. "Most of my family has. Pop was raised there."

"Pop?" I said. "You call your dad Pop?"

"Yeppers."

I let out a puff and checked the clock. Less than three hours until lunch.

DON'T MISS THE OTHER ADVENTURES OF RIP AND RED!